William Makepeace Thackeray

The Complete Poems of W. M. Thackeray

Vol. 1

William Makepeace Thackeray

The Complete Poems of W. M. Thackeray
Vol. 1

ISBN/EAN: 9783337408244

Printed in Europe, USA, Canada, Australia, Japan

Cover: Foto ©Andreas Hilbeck / pixelio.de

More available books at **www.hansebooks.com**

THE

COMPLETE POEMS

OF

W. M. THACKERAY

NEW YORK

WHITE, STOKES, AND ALLEN

1886

ADVERTISEMENT.

This edition of Mr. Thackeray's poems will be found to include all the verses that are scattered throughout the author's various writings.

CONTENTS.

LOVE-SONGS MADE EASY.

FIVE GERMAN DITTIES.

BALLADS.

THE CHRONICLE OF THE DRUM.

PART I.

At Paris, hard by the Maine barriers,
  Whoever will choose to repair,
Midst a dozen of wooden-legged warriors
  May haply fall in with old Pierre.
On the sunshiny bench of a tavern
  He sits and he prates of old wars,
And moistens his pipe of tobacco
  With a drink that is named after Mars.

The beer makes his tongue run the quicker,
  And as long as his tap never fails
Thus over his favorite liquor
  Old Peter will tell his old tales.
Says he, " In my life's ninety summers
  Strange changes and chances I've seen,—
So here's to all gentlemen drummers
  That ever have thumped on a skin.

" Brought up in the art military
  For four generations we are ;
My ancestors drumm'd for King Harry,
  The Huguenot lad of Navarre.
And as each man in life has his station
  According as Fortune may fix,
While Condé was waving the bâton,
  My grandsire was trolling the sticks.

"Ah ! those were the days for commanders !
    What glories my grandfather won,
Ere bigots, and lackeys, and panders
    The fortunes of France had undone !
In Germany, Flanders, and Holland,—
    What foeman resisted us then ?
No ; my grandsire was ever victorious,
    My grandsire and Monsieur Turenne.

" He died : and our noble battalions
    The jade fickle Fortune forsook ;
And at Blenheim, in spite of our valiance,
    The victory lay with Malbrook.
The news it was brought to King Louis ;
    Corbleu ! how his Majesty swore
When he heard they had taken my grandsire :
    And twelve thousand gentlemen more.

" At Namur, Ramillies, and Malplaquet
    Were we posted, on plain or in trench :
Malbrook only need to attack it
    And away from him scamper'd we French.
Cheer up ! 'tis no use to be glum, boys,—
    'Tis written, since fighting begun,
That sometimes we fight and we conquer,
    And sometimes we fight and we run.

" To fight and to run was our fate :
    Our fortune and fame had departed.
And so perish'd Louis the Great,—
    Old, lonely, and half broken-hearted.
His coffin they pelted with mud,
    His body they tried to lay hands on ;
And so having buried King Louis
    They loyally served his great-grandson.

" God save the beloved King Louis !
    (For so he was nicknamed by some,)

And now came my father to do his
    King's orders and beat on the drum.
My grandsire was dead, but his bones
    Must have shaken, I'm certain, for joy,
To hear daddy drumming the English
    From the meadows of famed Fontenoy.

"So well did he drum in that battle
    That the enemy show'd us their backs;
Corbleu! it was pleasant to rattle
    The sticks and to follow old Saxe!
We next had Soubise as a leader,
    And as luck hath its changes and fits,
At Rosbach, in spite of dad's drumming,
    'Tis said we were beaten by Fritz.

"And now daddy cross'd the Atlantic,
    To drum for Montcalm and his men;
Morbleu! but it makes a man frantic
    To think we were beaten again!
My daddy he cross'd the wide ocean,
    My mother brought me on her neck,
And we came in the year fifty-seven
    To guard the good town of Quebec.

"In the year fifty-nine came the Britons,—
    Full well I remember the day,—
They knocked at our gates for admittance,
    Their vessels were moor'd in our bay.
Says our general, 'Drive me yon red-coats
    Away to the sea whence they come!'
So we march'd against Wolfe and his bull-dogs,
    We marched at the sound of the drum.

"I think I can see my poor mammy
    With me in her hand as she waits,
And our regiment, slowly retreating,
    Pours back through the citadel gates.

Dear mammy she looks in their faces,
    And asks if her husband is come?
—He is lying all cold on glacis,
    And will never more beat on the drum.

"Come, drink, 'tis no use to be glum, boys!
    He died like a soldier in glory;
Here's a glass to the health of all drum-boys,
    And now I'll commence my own story.
Once more did we cross the salt ocean,
    We came in the year eighty-one;
And the wrongs of my father the drummer
    Were avenged by the drummer his son.

"In Chesapeake Bay we were landed.
    In vain strove the British to pass:
Rochambeau our armies commanded,
    Our ships they were led by De Grasse.
Morbleu! how I rattled the drumsticks
    The day we march'd into Yorktown;
Ten thousand of beef-eating British
    Their weapons we caused to lay down.

"Then homewards returning victorious,
    In peace to our country we came,
And were thanked for our glorious actions
    By Louis, Sixteenth of the name.
What drummer on earth could be prouder
    Than I, while I drumm'd at Versailles
To the lovely court ladies in powder,
    And lappets, and long satin-tails?

"The princes that day pass'd before us,
    Our countrymen's glory and hope;
Monsieur, who was learned in Horace,
    D'Artois, who could dance the tight-rope
One night we kept guard for the Queen
    At her Majesty's opera-box,

While the King, that majestical monarch,
    Sat filing at home at his locks.

"Yes, I drumm'd for the fair Antoinette,
    And so smiling she look'd and so tender,
That our officers, privates, and drummers,
    All vow'd they would die to defend her.
But she cared not for us honest fellows,
    Who fought and who bled in her wars,
She sneer'd at our gallant Rochambeau,
    And turned Lafayette out of doors.

"Ventrebleu ! then I swore a great oath,
    No more to such tyrants to kneel ;
And so, just to keep up my drumming,
    One day I drumm'd down the Bastille,
Ho, landlord ! a stoup of fresh wine.
    Come, comrades, a bumper we'll try,
And drink to the year eighty-nine
    And the glorious fourth of July !

"Then bravely our cannon it thunder'd
    As onwards our patriots bore.
Our enemies were but a hundred,
    And we twenty thousand or more.
They carried the news to King Louis.
    He heard it as calm as you please,
And, like a majestical monarch,
    Kept filing his locks and his keys.

"We show'd our republican courage,
    We storm'd and we broke the great gate in,
And we murder'd the insolent governor
    For daring to keep us a-waiting.
Lambesc and his squadrons stood by :
    They never stirr'd finger or thumb.
The saucy aristocrats trembled
    As they heard the republican drum.

"Hurrah ! what a storm was a-brewing !
   The day of our vengeance was come !
Through scenes of what carnage and ruin
   Did I beat on the patriot drum !
Let's drink to the famed tenth of August :
   At midnight I beat the tattoo,
And woke up the pikemen of Paris
   To follow the bold Barbaroux.

" With pikes, and with shouts, and with torches
   March'd onwards our dusty battalions,
And we girt the tall castle of Louis,
   A million of tatterdemalions !
We storm'd the fair gardens where tower'd
   The walls of his heritage splendid.
Ah, shame on him, craven and coward,
   That had not the heart to defend it !

" With the crown of his sires on his head,
   His nobles and knights by his side,
At the foot of his ancestors' palace
   'Twere easy, methinks, to have died.
But no : when we burst through his barriers,
   Mid heaps of the dying and dead,
In vain through the chambers we sought him—
   He had turn'd like a craven and fled.

        *   *   *   *   *

" You all know the Place de la Concorde ?
   'Tis hard by the Tuileries wall,
Mid terraces, fountains, and statues,
   There rises an obelisk tall.
There rises an obelisk tall,
   All garnish'd and gilded the base is :
'Tis surely the gayest of all
   Our beautiful city's gay places.

" Around it are gardens and flowers,
    And the Cities of France on their thrones,
Each crown'd with his circlet of flowers
    Sits watching this biggest of stones !
I love to go sit in the sun there,
    The flowers and fountains to see,
And to think of the deeds that were done there
    In the glorious year ninety-three.

" 'Twas here stood the Altar of Freedom ;
    And though neither marble nor gilding
Was used in those days to adorn
    Our simple republican building,
Corbleu ! but the MÈRE GUILLOTINE
    Cared little for splendour or show,
So you gave her an axe and a beam,
    And a plank and a basket or so.

" Awful, and proud, and erect,
    Here sat our republican goddess.
Each morning her table we deck'd
    With dainty aristocrats' bodies.
The people each day flocked around
    As she sat at her meat and her wine :
'Twas always the use of our nation
    To witness the sovereign dine.

" Young virgins with fair golden tresses,
    Old silver-hair'd prelates and priests,
Dukes, marquises, barons, princesses,
    Were splendidly served at her feasts.
Ventrebleu ! but we pamper'd our ogress
    With the best that our nation could bring,
And dainty she grew in her progress,
    And called for the head of a King !

" She called for the blood of our King,
    And straight from his prison we drew him ;

And to her with shouting we led him,
    And took him, and bound him, and slew him.
‘ The Monarchs of Europe against me
    Have plotted a godless alliance :
I’ll fling them the head of King Louis,’
    She said, ‘ as my gage of defiance.’

“ I see him as now, for a moment,
    Away from his gaolers he broke ;
And stood at the foot of the scaffold,
    And linger’d, and fain would have spoke.
‘ Ho, drummer ! quick, silence yon Capet.’
    Says Santerre, ‘ with a beat of your drum.’
Lustily then did I tap it,
    And the son of Saint Louis was dumb.

      *   *   *   *   *

PART II.

“ The glorious days of September
    Saw many aristocrats fall ;
’Twas then that our pikes drank the blood
    In the beautiful breast of Lamballe.
Pardi, ’twas a beautiful lady !
    I seldom have look’d on her like ;
And I drumm’d for a gallant procession,
    That march’d with her head on a pike.

“ Let’s show the pale head to the Queen,
    We said—she’ll remember it well.
She looked from the bars of her prison,
    And shrieked as she saw it, and fell.
We set up a shout at her screaming,
    We laugh’d at the fright she had shown
At the sight of the head of her minion—
    How she’d tremble to part with her own !

" We had taken the head of King Capet,
   We called for the blood of his wife ;
Undaunted she came to the scaffold,
   And bared her fair neck to the knife.
As she felt the foul fingers that touch'd her,
   She shrank, but she deigned not to speak :
She look'd with a royal disdain,
   And died with a blush on her cheek !

" 'Twas thus that our country was saved ;
   So told us the safety committee,
But psha ! I've the heart of a soldier,
   All gentleness, mercy, and pity.
I loath'd to assist at such deeds,
   And my drum beat its loudest of tunes
As we offered to justice offended
   The blood of the bloody tribunes.

" Away with such foul recollections !
   No more of the axe and the block ;
I saw the last fight of the sections,
   As they fell 'neath our guns at Saint Rock.
Young BONAPARTE led us that day ;
   When he sought the Italian frontier,
I follow'd the gallant young captain,
   I follow'd him many a long year.

" We came to an army in rags,
   Our general was but a boy
When we first saw the Austrain flags
   Flaunt proud in the fields of Savoy.
In the glorious year ninety-six,
   We march'd to the banks of the Po ;
I carried my drum and my sticks,
   And we laid the proud Austrian low.

" In triumph we enter'd Milan,
   We seized on the Mantuan keys ;

The troops of the Emperor ran,
　And the Pope he fell down on his knees."—
Pierre's comrades here call'd a fresh bottle,
　And clubbing together their wealth,
They drank to the Army of Italy,
　And General Bonaparte's health.

The drummer now bared his old breast,
　And show'd us a plenty of scars,
Rude presents that Fortune had made him
　In fifty victorious wars.
' This came when I follow'd bold Kleber—
　'Twas shot by a Mameluke gun ;
And this from an Austrian sabre,
　When the field of Marengo was won.

" My forehead has many deep furrows,
　But this is the deepest of all :
A Brunswicker made it at Jena,
　Beside the fair river of Saal.
This cross, 'twas the Emperor gave it ;
　(God bless him !) it covers a blow ;
I had it at Austerlitz fight,
　As I beat on my drum in the snow.

" 'Twas thus that we conquer'd and fought ;
　But wherefore continue the story ?
There's never a baby in France
　But has heard of our chief and our glory,—
But has heard of our chief and our fame,
　His sorrows and triumphs can tell,
How bravely Napoleon conquer'd,
　How bravely and sadly he fell.

" It makes my old heart to beat higher,
　To think of the deeds that I saw ;
I follow'd bold Ney through the fire,
　And charged at the side of Murat."

And so did old Peter continue
  His story of twenty brave years ;
His audience follow'd with comments—
  Rude comments of curses and tears.

He told how the Prussians in vain
  Had died in defence of their land ;
His audience laugh'd at the story,
  And vowed that their captain was grand !
He had fought the red English, he said,
  In many a battle of Spain :
They cursed the red English, and prayed
  To meet them and fight them again.

He told them how Russia was lost,
  Had winter not driven them back ;
And his company cursed the quick frost
  And doubly they cursed the Cossack.
He told how the stranger arrived ;
  They wept at the tale of disgrace ;
And they long'd but for one battle more,
  The stain of their shame to efface.

" Our country their hordes overrun,
  We fled to the fields of Champagne,
And fought them, though twenty to one.
  And beat them again and again !
Our warrior was conquer'd at last ;
  They bade him his crown to resign ;
To fate and his country he yielded
  The rights of himself and his line.

" He came, and among us he stood,
  Around him we press'd in a throng :
We could not regard him for weeping,
  Who had led us and loved us so long.
'I have led you for twenty long years,'
  Napoleon said ere he went ;

' Wherever was honor I found you,
  And with you, my sons, am content !

" ' Though Europe against me was armed,
    Your chiefs and my people are true ;
  I still might have struggled with fortune,
    And baffled all Europe with you.

" ' But France would have suffer'd the while,
    'Tis best that I suffer alone ;
  I go to my place of exile,
    To write of the deeds we have done.

" ' Be true to the king that they give you.
    We may not embrace ere we part ;
  But, General, reach me your hand,
    And press me, I pray, to your heart.'

" He call'd for our battle standard ;
    One kiss to the eagle he gave.
  ' Dear eagle ! ' he said, ' may this kiss
    Long sound in the hearts of the brave ! '
  'Twas thus that Napoleon left us ;
    Our people were weeping and mute,
  As he passed through the lines of his guard,
    And our drums beat the notes of salute.

                *   *   *   *   *

" I look'd when the drumming was o'er,
    I look'd, but our hero was gone ;
  We were destined to see him once more,
    When we fought on the Mount of St. John.
  The Emperor rode through our files ;
    'Twas June, and a fair Sunday morn,
  The lines of our warriors for miles
    Stretch'd wide through the Waterloo corn.

" In thousands we stood on the plain,
    The red-coats were crowning the height ;
' Go scatter yon English,' he said ;
    ' We'll sup, lads, at Brussels to-night.'
We answer'd his voice with a shout ;
    Our eagles were bright in the sun ;
Our drums and our cannon spoke out,
    And the thundering battle begun.

"One charge to another succeeds,
    Like waves that a hurricane bears ;
All day do our galloping steeds
    Dash fierce on the enemy's squares.
At noon we began the fell onset :
    We charged up the Englishmen's hill ;
And madly we charged it at sunset—
    His banners were floating there still.

" —Go to ! I will tell you no more ;
    You know how the battle was lost.
Ho ! fetch me a beaker of wine,
    And, comrades, I'll give you a toast.
I'll give you a curse on all traitors,
    Who plotted our Emperor's ruin ;
And a curse on those red-coated English,
    Whose bayonets helped our undoing.

" A curse on those British assassins,
    Who order'd the slaughter of Ney ;
A curse on Sir Hudson, who tortured
    The life of our hero away.
A curse on all Russians—I hate them—
    On all Prussian and Austrian fry ;
And oh ! but I pray we may meet them,
    And fight them again ere I die."

'Twas thus old Peter did conclude
    His chronicle with curses fit.

He spoke the tale in accents rude,
  In ruder verse I copied it.

Perhaps the tale a moral bears,
  (All tales in time to this must come,)
The story of two hundred years
  Writ on the parchment of a drum.

What Peter told with drum and stick,
  Is endless theme for poet's pen :
Is found in endless quartos thick,
  Enormous books by learned men.

And ever since historian writ,
  And ever since a bard could sing,
Doth each exalt with all his wit
  The noble art of murdering.

We love to read the glorious page,
  How bold Achilles killed his foe ;
And Turnus, felled by Trojans' rage,
  Went howling to the shades below.

How Godfrey led his red-cross knights,
  How mad Orlando slash'd and slew ;
There's not a single bard that writes
  But doth the glorious theme renew.

And while, in fashion picturesque,
  The poet rhymes of blood and blows,
The grave historian at his desk
  Describes the same in classic prose.

Go read the works of Reverend Coxe,
  You'll duly see recorded there
The history of the self-same knocks
  Here roughly sung by Drummer Pierre.

Of battles fierce and warriors big,
   He writes in phrases dull and slow,
And waves his cauliflower wig,
   And shouts "Saint George for Marlborow !"

Take Doctor Southey from the shelf,
   An LL.D.,—a peaceful man ;
Good Lord, how doth he plume himself
   Because we beat the Corsican !

From first to last his page is filled
   With stirring tales how blows were struck.
He shows how we the Frenchmen kill'd,
   And praises God for our good luck.

Some hints, 'tis true, of politics
   The doctors give and statesman's art :
Pierre only bangs his drum and sticks,
   And understands the bloody part.

He cares not what the cause may be,
   He is not nice for wrong and right ;
But show him where's the enemy,
   He only asks to drum and fight.

They bid him fight,—perhaps he wins ;
   And when he tells the story o'er,
The honest savage brags and grins,
   And only longs to fight once more.

But luck may change, and valor fail,
   Our drummer, Peter, meet reverse,
And with a moral points his tale—
   The end of all such tales—a curse.

Last year, my love, it was my hap
   Behind a grenadier to be,

And, but he wore a hairy cap,
   No taller man, methinks, than me.

Prince Albert and the Queen, God wot,
   (Be blessings on the glorious pair !)
Before us passed. I saw them not—
   I only saw a cap of hair.

Your orthodox historian puts
   In foremost rank the soldier thus,
The red-coat bully in his boots,
   That hides the march of men from us.

He puts them there in foremost rank,
   You wonder at his cap of hair :
You hear his sabre's cursed clank,
   His spurs are jingling everywhere.

Go to ! I hate him and his trade :
   Who bade us so to cringe and bend
And all God's peaceful people made
   To such as him subservient ?

Tell me what find we to admire
   In epaulets and scarlet coats—
In men, because they load and fire,
   And know the art of cutting throats ?

    *   *   *   *   *

Ah, gentle, tender lady mine !
   The winter wind blows cold and shrill ;
Come, fill me one more glass of wine,
   And give the silly fools their will.

And what care we for war and wrack,
   How kings and heroes rise and fall ?

Look yonder,* in his coffin black
  There lies the greatest of them all !

To pluck him down, and keep him up,
  Died many million human souls.—
'Tis twelve o'clock and time to sup ;
  Bid Mary heap the fire with coals.

He captured many thousand guns ;
  He wrote " The Great" before his name ;
And dying, only left his sons
  The recollection of his shame.

Though more than half the world was his,
  He died without a rood his own ;
And borrow'd from his enemies
  Six foot of ground to lie upon.

He fought a thousand glorious wars,
  And more than half the world was his,
And somewhere now, in yonder stars,
  Can tell, mayhap, what greatness is.
1841.

———

ABD-EL-KADER AT TOULON.

OR, THE CAGED HAWK.

No more, thou lithe and long-winged hawk, of
  desert life for thee ;
No more across the sultry sands shalt thou go
  swooping free :

---

* This ballad was written at Paris at the time of the
Second Funeral of Napoleon.

Blunt idle talons, idle beak, with spurning of thy
  chain,
Shatter against thy cage the wing thou ne'er
  may'st spread again.

Long, sitting by their watchfires, shall the Ka-
  byles tell the tale
Of thy dash from Ben Halifa on the fat Metidja
  vale ;
How thou swept'st the desert over, bearing down
  the wild El Riff,
From eastern Beni Salah to western Ouad Shelif ;

How thy white burnous went streaming, like the
  storm-rack o'er the sea,
When thou rodest in the vanward of the Moorish
  chivalry ;
How thy razzia was a whirlwind, thy onset a
  simoom,
How thy sword-sweep was the lightning, dealing
  death from out the gloom !

Nor less quick to slay in battle than in peace to
  spare and save,
Of brave men wisest councillor, of wise councillors most brave ;
How the eye that flashed destruction could beam
  gentleness and love,
How lion in thee mated lamb, how eagle mated
  dove !

Availèd not or steel or shot 'gainst that charmèd
  life secure,
Till cunning France, in last resource, tossed up
  the golden lure ;
And the carrion buzzards round him stooped,
  faithless, to the cast,

And the wild hawk of the desert is caught and
caged at last.

Weep, maidens of Zerifah, above the laden loom !
Scar, chieftains of Al Elmah, your cheeks in grief
and gloom !
Sons of the Beni Snazam, throw down the useless
lance,
And stoop your necks and bare your backs to
yoke and scourge of France !

'Twas not in fight they bore him down ; he never
cried *amàn ;*
He never sank his sword before the PRINCE OF
FRANGHISTAN ;
But with traitors all around him, his star upon
the wane,
He heard the voice of ALLAH, and he would not
strive in vain.

They gave him what he asked them ; from king
to king he spake,
As one that plighted word and seal not knoweth
how to break :
" Let me pass from out my deserts, be't mine
own choice where to go ;
I brook no fettered life to live, a captive and a
show."

And they promised, and he trusted them, and
proud and calm he came,
Upon his black mare riding, girt with his sword
of fame.
Good steed, good sword, he rendered both unto
the Frankish throng ;
He knew them false and fickle—but a Prince's
word is strong.

How have they kept their promise ?   Turned they
   the vessel's prow
Unto Acre, Alexandria, as they have sworn e'en
   now ?
Not so : from Oran northwards the white sails
   gleam and glance,
And the wild hawk of the desert is borne away to
   France !

Where Toulon's white-walled lazaret looks south-
   ward o'er the wave,
Sits he that trusted in the word a son of Louis
   gave.
O noble faith of noble heart !   And was the warn-
   ing vain,
The text writ by the Bourbon in the blurred
   black book of Spain?

They have need of thee to gaze on, they have
   need of thee to grace
The triumph of the Prince, to gild the pinchbeck
   of their race.
Words are but wind, conditions must be con-
   strued by Guizot ;
Dash out thy heart, thou desert hawk, ere thou
   art made a show !

THE KING OF BRENTFORD'S TESTA-
MENT.

The noble King of Brentford
   Was old and very sick,
He summon'd his physicians
   To wait upon him quick ;

They stepp'd into their coaches
And brought their best physick.

They cramm'd their gracious master
With potion and with pill ;
They drench'd him and they bled him :
They could not cure his ill.
"Go fetch," says he, "my lawyer ;
I'd better make my will."

The monarch's royal mandate
The lawyer did obey ;
The thought of six-and-eight-pence
Did make his heart full gay.
"What is't," says he, "your Majesty
Would wish of me to-day ?"

"The doctors have belabor'd me
With potion and with pill :
My hours of life are counted,
O man of tape and quill !
Sit down and mend a pen or two ;
I want to make my will.

"O'er all the land of Brentford
I'm lord, and eke of Kew :
I've three-per-cents and five-per-cents :
My debts are but a few ;
And to inherit after me
I have but children two.

"Prince Thomas is my eldest son ;
A sober prince is he,
And from the day we breech'd him
Till now—he's twenty-three—
He never caused disquiet
To his poor mamma or me.

" At school they never flogg'd him ;
  At college, though not fast,
Yet his little-go and great-go
  He creditably pass'd,
And made his year's allowance
  For eighteen months to last.

" He never owed a shilling,
  Went never drunk to bed,
He has not two ideas
  Within his honest head—
In all respects he differs
  From my second son, Prince Ned.

" When Tom has half his income
  Laid by at the year's end,
Poor Ned has ne'er a stiver
  That rightly he may spend,
But sponges on a tradesman,
  Or borrows from a friend.

" While Tom his legal studies
  Most soberly pursues,
Poor Ned must pass his mornings
  A-dawdling with the Muse :
While Tom frequents his banker,
  Young Ned frequents the Jews.

" Ned drives about in buggies,
  Tom sometimes takes a 'bus ;
Ah, cruel fate, why made you
  My children differ thus ?
Why make of Tom a *dullard*,
  And Ned a *genius ?*"

" You'll cut him with a shilling,"
  Exclaimed the man of wits :

" I'll leave my wealth," said Brentford,
    " Sir Lawyer, as befits,
And portion both their fortunes
    Unto their several wits."

" Your Grace knows best," the lawyer said,
    " On your commands I wait."
" Be silent, Sir," says Brentford,
    " A plague upon your prate !
Come take your pen and paper,
    And write as I dictate."

The will as Brentford spoke it
    Was writ and signed and closed ;
He bade the lawyer leave him,
    And turn'd him round and dozed ;
And next week in the churchyard
    The good old King reposed.

Tom, dressed in crape and hatband,
    Of mourners was the chief ;
In bitter self-upraidings
    Poor Edward showed his grief :
Tom hid his fat white countenance
    In his pocket-handkerchief.

Ned's eyes were full of weeping,
    He falter'd in his walk ;
Tom never shed a tear,
    But onwards he did stalk,
As pompous, black, and solemn
    As any catafalque.

And when the bones of Brentford—
    That gentle king and just—
With bell and book and candle
    Were duly laid in dust,

" Now, gentlemen," says Thomas,
" Let business be discussed.

" When late our sire beloved
　　Was taken deadly ill,
Sir Lawyer, you attended him
　　(I mean to tax your bill) ;
And, as you signed and wrote it,
　　I prithee read the will."

The lawyer wiped his spectacles,
　　And drew the parchment out ;
And all the Brentford family
　　Sat eager round about :
Poor Ned was somewhat anxious,
　　But Tom had ne'er a doubt.

" My son, as I make ready
　　To seek my last long home,
Some cares I had for Neddy,
　　But none for thee, my Tom :
Sobriety and order
　　You ne'er departed from.

" Ned hath a brilliant genius,
　　And thou a plodding brain ;
On thee I think with pleasure,
　　On him with doubt and pain."
(" You see, good Ned," says Thomas,
　　" What he thought about us twain.")

" Though small was your allowance,
　　You saved a little store ;
And those who save a little
　　Shall get a plenty more."
As the lawyer read this compliment,
　　Tom's eyes were running o'er.

" The tortoise and the hare, Tom,
 Set out at each his pace ;
The hare it was the fleeter,
 The tortoise won the race ;
And since the world's beginning
 This ever was the case.

" Ned's genius, blithe and singing,
 Steps gaily o'er the ground ;
As steadily you trudge it,
 He clears it with a bound ;
But dulness has stout legs, Tom,
 And wind that's wondrous sound.

" O'er fruits and flowers alike, Tom,
 You pass with plodding feet ;
You heed not one nor t'other,
 But onwards go your beat ;
While genius stops to loiter
 With all that he may meet ;

" And ever as he wanders,
 Will have a pretext fine
For sleeping in the morning,
 Or loitering to dine,
Or dozing in the shade,
 Or basking in the shine.

" Your little steady eyes, Tom,
 Though not so bright as those
That restless round about him
 His flashing genius throws,
Are excellently suited
 To look before your nose.

" Thank heaven, then, for the blinkers
 It placed before your eyes ;

The stupidest are strongest,
    The witty are not wise ;
Oh, bless your good stupidity !
    It is your dearest prize.

" And though my lands are wide,
    And plenty is my gold
Still better gifts from Nature,
    My Thomas, do you hold—
A brain that's thick and heavy,
    A heart that's dull and cold.

" Too dull to feel depression,
    Too hard to heed distress,
Too cold to yield to passion
    Or silly tenderness.
March on—your road is open
    To wealth, Tom, and success.

" Ned sinneth in extravagance,
    And you in greedy lust."
(" I' faith," says Ned, " our father
    Is less polite than just.")
" In you, son Tom, I've confidence,
    But Ned I cannot trust."

" Wherefore my lease and copyholds,
    My lands and tenements,
My parks, my farms, and orchards,
    My houses and my rents,
My Dutch stock and my Spanish stock,
    My five and three per cents,

" I leave to you, my Thomas"—
    (" What, all ?" poor Edward said.
" Well, well, I should have spent them,
    And Tom's a prudent head ")—

" I leave to you, my Thomas,—
  To you IN TRUST for Ned."

The wrath and consternation
  What poet e'er could trace
That at this fatal passage
  Came o'er Prince Tom his face ;
The wonder of the company,
  And honest Ned's amaze ?

" 'Tis surely some mistake,"
  Good-naturedly cries Ned ;
The lawyer answered gravely,
  " 'Tis even as I said ;
'Twas thus his gracious Majesty
  Ordain'd on his death-bed.

" See, here the will is witness'd,
  And here's his autograph."
" In truth, our father's writing,"
  Says Edward, with a laugh ;
" But thou shalt not be a loser, Tom ¡
  We'll share it half and half."

" Alas ! my kind young gentleman,
  This sharing cannot be ;
'Tis written in the testament
  That Brentford spoke to me,
' I do forbid Prince Ned to give.
  Prince Tom a halfpenny.

" ' He hath a store of money,
  But ne'er was known to lend it ;
He never helped his brother ;
  The poor he ne'er befriended ;
He hath no need of property
  Who knows not how to spend it.

"' Poor Edward knows but how to spend,
  And thrifty Tom to hoard ;
Let Thomas be the steward then,
  And Edward be the lord ;
And as the honest laborer
  Is worthy his reward,

"' I pray Prince Ned, my second son,
  And my successor dear,
To pay to his intendant
  Five hundred pounds a year ;
And to think of his old father,
  And live and make good cheer.'"

Such was old Brentford's honest testament,
  He did devise his moneys for the best,
And lies in Brentford church in peaceful rest.
Prince Edward lived, and money made and spent ;
  But his good sire was wrong, it is confess'd,
To say his son, young Thomas, never lent.
  He did.   Young Thomas lent at interest,
And nobly took his twenty-five per cent.

Long time the famous reign of Ned endured
  O'er Chiswick, Fulham, Brentford, Putney, Kew,
But of extravagance he ne'er was cured.
  And when both died, as mortal men will do,
'Twas commonly reported that the steward
  Was very much the richer of the two.

THE WHITE SQUALL.

On deck, beneath the awning,
I dozing lay and yawning ;
It was the gray of dawning,
  Ere yet the sun arose ;

And above the funnel's roaring,
And the fitful winds deploring,
I heard the cabin snoring
    With universal nose.
I could hear the passengers snorting,
I envied their disporting—
Vainly I was courting
    The pleasure of a doze !

So I lay, and wondered why light
Came not, and watched the twilight,
And the glimmer of the skylight,
    That shot across the deck,
And the binnacle pale and steady,
And the dull glimpse of the dead-eye,
And the sparks in fiery eddy
    That whirled from the chimney neck.
In our jovial floating prison
There was sleep from fore to mizzen,
And never a star had risen
    The hazy sky to speck.

Strange company we harbored ;
We'd a hundred Jews to larboard,
Unwashed, uncombed, unbarbered—
    Jews black, and brown, and gray ;
With terror it would seize ye,
And make your souls uneasy,
To see those Rabbis greasy,
    Who did nought but scratch and pray :
Their dirty children puking—
Their dirty saucepans cooking—
Their dirty fingers hooking
    Their swarming fleas away.

To starboard, Turks and Greeks were—
Whiskered and brown their cheeks were—

Enormous wide their breeks were,
  Their pipes did puff alway ;
Each on his mat allotted
In silence smoked and squatted,
Whilst round their children trotted
  In pretty, pleasant play.
He can't but smile who traces
The smiles on those brown faces,
And the pretty prattling graces
  Of those small heathens gay.

And so the hours kept tolling,
And through the ocean rolling
Went the brave " Iberia" bowling
  Before the break of day—

When A SQUALL, upon a sudden,
Came o'er the waters scudding ;
And the clouds began to gather,
And the sea was lashed to lather,
And the lowering thunder grumbled,
And the lightning jumped and tumbled,
And the ship, and all the ocean,
Woke up in wild commotion.
Then the wind set up a howling,
And the poodle dog a yowling,
And the cocks began a crowing,
And the old cow raised a lowing,
As she heard the tempest blowing ;
And fowls and geese did cackle,
And the cordage and the tackle
Began to shriek and cackle ;
And the spray dashed o'er the funnels,
And down the deck in runnels ;
And the rushing water soaks all,
From the seamen in the fo'ksal
To the stokers whose black faces

Peer out of their bed places ;
And the captain he was bawling,
And the sailors pulling, hauling,
And the quarter-deck tarpauling
Was shivered in the squalling ;
And the passengers awaken,
Most pitifully shaken ;
And the steward jumps up, and hastens
For the necessary basins.

Then the Greeks they groaned and quivered,
And they knelt, and moaned, and shivered,
As the plunging waters met them
And splashed and overset them ;
And they call in their emergence
Upon countless saints and virgins ;
And their marrowbones are bended,
And they think the world is ended.
And the Turkish women for'ard
Were frightened and behorror'd ;
And shrieking and bewildering,
The mothers clutched their children ;
The men sang " Allah ! Illah !
Mashallah Bismillah !"
As the warring waters doused them,
And splashed them and soused them,
And they called upon the Prophet,
And thought but little of it.

Then all the fleas in Jewry
Jumped up and bit like fury ;
And the progeny of Jacob
Did on the main-deck wake up
(I wot those greasy Rabbins
Would never pay for cabins) ;
And each man moaned and jabbered in
His filthy Jewish gaberdine,

In woe and lamentation,
And howling consternation.
And the splashing water drenches
Their dirty brats and wenches ;
And they crawl from bales and benches
In a hundred thousand stenches.

This was the White Squall famous,
Which latterly o'ercame us,
And which all will well remember
On the 28th September ;
When a Prussian captain of Lancers
(Those tight-laced, whiskered prancers)
Came on the deck astonished,
By that wild squall admonished,
And wondering cried, " Potztausend !
Wie ist der Sturm jetzt brausend !"
And looked at Captain Lewis,
Who calmly stood and blew his
Cigar in all the bustle,
And scorned the tempest's tussle.
And oft we've thought thereafter
How he beat the storm to laughter ;
For well he knew his vessel
With that vain wind could wrestle ;
And when a wreck we thought her,
And doomed ourselves to slaughter,
How gaily he fought her,
And though the hubbub brought her,
And as the tempest caught her,
Cried, "GEORGE ! SOME BRANDY-AND-
WATER !"

And when, its force expended,
The harmless storm was ended,
And as the sunrise splendid
Came blushing o'er the sea,

I thought, as day was breaking,
My little girls were waking,
And smiling, and making
A prayer at home for me.

1844.

————

PEG OF LIMAVADDY.

RIDING from Coleraine
  (Famed for lovely Kitty),
Came a Cockney bound
  Unto Derry city;
Weary was his soul,
  Shivering and sad, he
Bumped along the road
  Leads to Limavaddy.

Mountains stretch'd around,
  Gloomy was their tinting,
And the horse's hoofs
  Made a dismal clinting;
Wind upon the heath
  Howling was and piping,
On the heath and bog,
  Black with many a snipe in.
Mid the bogs of black,
  Silver pools were flashing,
Crows upon their sides
  Pecking were and splashing.
Cockney on the car
  Closer folds his plaidy,
Grumbling at the road
  Leads to Limavaddy.

Through the crashing woods
  Autumn brawl'd and blustered,
Tossing round about
  Leaves the hue of mustard;
Yonder lay Lough Foyle,
  Which a storm was whipping,
Covering with the mist
  Lake, and shores, and shipping.
Up and down the hill
  (Nothing could be bolder),
Horse went with a raw
  Bleeding on his shoulder.
" Where are horses changed ?"
  Said I to the laddy
Driving on the box :
  " Sir, at Limavaddy."

Limavaddy inn's
  But a humble bait-house,
Where you may procure
  Whiskey and potatoes ;
Landlord at the door
  Gives a smiling welcome
To the shivering wights
  Who to this hotel come.
Landlady within
  Sits and knits a stocking,
With a wary foot
  Baby's cradle rocking.

To the chimney nook
  Having found admittance,
There I watch a pup
  Playing with two kittens ;
(Playing round the fire,
  Which of blazing turf is,
Roaring to the pot

Which bubbles with the murphies.)
And the cradled babe
   Fond the mother nursed it,
Singing it a song
   As she twists the worsted !

Up and down the stair
   Two more young ones patter
(Twins were never seen
   Dirtier or fatter).
Both have mottled legs,
   Both have snubby noses,
Both have—Here the host
   Kindly interposes :
" Sure you must be froze
   With the sleet and hail, sir :
So will you have some punch,
   Or will you have some ale, sir ?"

Presently a maid
   Enters with the liquor
(Half a pint of ale
   Frothing in a beaker).
Gads ! I didn't know
   What my beating heart meant :
Hebe's self, I thought,
   Entered the apartment.
As she came she smiled,
   And the smile bewitching,
On my word and honor,
   Lighted all the kitchen !
With a curtsey neat
   Greeting the new comer,
Lovely, smiling Peg
   Offers me the rummer ;

But my trembling hand
   Up the beaker tilted.

And the glass of ale
    Every drop I spilt it :
Spilt it every drop
    (Dames, who read my volumes,
Pardon such a word)
    On my what-d'ye-call-'ems !

Witnessing the sight
    Of that dire disaster,
Out began to laugh
    Missis, maid, and master ;
Such a merry peal
    'Specially Miss Peg's was,
(As the glass of ale
    Trickling down my legs was,)
That the joyful sound
    Of that mingling laughter
Echoed in my ears
    Many a long day after.

Such a silver peal !
    In the meadows listening,
You who've heard the bells
    Ringing to a christening ;
You who ever heard
    Caradori pretty,
Smiling like an angel,
    Singing " Giovinetti ;"
Fancy Peggy's laugh,
    Sweet, and clear, and cheerful,
At my pantaloons
    With half a pint of beer full !

When the laugh was done,
    Peg, the pretty hussy,
Moved about the room
    Wonderfully busy ;

Now she looks to see
   If the kettle keeps hot ;
Now she rubs the spoons,
   Now she cleans the teapot ;
Now she sets the cups
   Trimly and secure :
Now she scours a pot,
   And so it was I drew her.

Thus it was I drew her
   Scouring of a kettle,
(Faith ! her blushing cheeks
   Redden'd on the metal !)
Ah ! but 'tis in vain
   That I try to sketch it ;
The pot perhaps is like,
   But Peggy's face is wretched.
No ! the best of lead
   And of india-rubber
Never could depict
   That sweet kettle-scrubber !

See her as she moves,
   Scarce the ground she touches
Airy as a fay,
   Graceful as a duchess :
Bare her rounded arm,
   Bare her little leg is,
Vestris never show'd
   Ankles like to Peggy's.
Braided is her hair,
   Soft her look and modest,
Slim her little waist
   Comfortably bodiced.

This I do declare,
   Happy is the laddy

Who the heart can share
  Of Peg of Limavaddy.
Married if she were,
  Blest would be the daddy
Of the children fair
  Of Peg of Limavaddy.
Beauty is not rare
  In the land of Paddy,
Fair beyond compare
  Is Peg of Limavaddy.

Citizen or Squire,
  Tory, Whig, or Radi-
cal would all desire
  Peg of Limavaddy.
Had I Homer's fire,
  Or that of Serjeant Taddy,
Meetly I'd admire
  Peg of Limavaddy.
And till I expire,
  Or till I grow mad, I
Will sing unto my lyre
  Peg of Limavaddy!

MAY-DAY ODE.

But yesterday a naked sod
  The dandies sneered from Rotten Row,
  And cantered o'er it to and fro:
    And see 'tis done!
As though 'twere by a wizard's rod
  A blazing arch of lucid glass
  Leaps like a fountain from the grass
    To meet the sun!

A quiet green but few days since,
　With cattle browsing in the shade :
And here are lines of bright arcade
　　　　　In order raised !
A palace as for fairy prince,
　A rare pavilion, such as man
Saw never since mankind began,
　　　　　And built and glazed !

A peaceful place it was but now,
　And lo ! within its shining streets
A multitude of nations meets ;
　　　　　A countless throng
I see beneath the crystal bow,
　And Gaul and German, Russ and Turk,
Each with his native handiwork
　　　　　And busy tongue.

I felt a thrill of love and awe
　To mark the different garb of each,
The changing tongue, the various speech
　　　　　Together blent :
A thrill, methinks, like His who saw
　" All people dwelling upon earth
Praising our God with solemn mirth
　　　　　And one consent."

High Sovereign, in your Royal state,
　Captains and chiefs, and councillors,
Before the lofty palace doors
　　　　　Are open set,—
Hush ! ere you pass the shining gate ;
　Hush ! ere the heaving curtain draws,
And let the Royal pageant pause
　　　　　A moment yet.

People and prince a silence keep !
  Bow coronet and kingly crown,
  Helmet and plume, bow lowly down,
        The while the priest,
Before the splendid portal step,
  (While still the wondrous banquet stays,)
  From Heaven supreme a blessing prays
        Upon the feast.

Then onwards let the triumph march ;
  Then let the loud artillery roll,
  And trumpets ring, and joy-bells toll,
        And pass the gate.
Pass underneath the shining arch,
  'Neath which the leafy elms are green ;
  Ascend unto your throne, O Queen !
        And take your state.

Behold her in her Royal place ;
  A gentle lady ; and the hand
  That sways the sceptre of this land,
        How frail and weak !
Soft is the voice, and fair the face :
  She breathes amen to prayer and hymn ;
  No wonder that her eyes are dim,
        And pale her cheek.

This moment round her empire's shores
  The winds of Austral winter sweep,
  And thousands lie in midnight sleep
        At rest to-day.
Oh ! awful is that crown of yours,
  Queen of innumerable realms
  Sitting beneath the budding elms
        Of English May !

A wondrous sceptre 'tis to bear :
  Strange mystery of God which set
  Upon her brow yon coronet,—
               The foremost crown
Of all the world, on one so fair !
  That chose her to it from her birth,
  And bade the sons of all the earth
               To her bow down.

The representatives of man
  Here from the far Antipodes,
  And from the subject Indian seas,
               In Congress meet ;
From Afric and from Hindustan,
  From Western continent and isle,
  The envoys of her empire pile
               Gifts at her feet ;

Our brethren cross the Atlantic tides,
  Loading the gallant decks which once
  Roared a defiance to our guns,
               With peaceful store ;
Symbol of peace, their vessel rides ! *
  O'er English waves float Star and Stripe,
  And firm their friendly anchors gripe
               The father shore !

From Rhine and Danube, Rhone and Seine,
  As rivers from their sources gush,
  The swelling floods of nations rush,
               And seaward pour :

From coast to coast in friendly chain,
  With countless ships we bridge the straits,
  And angry ocean separates
               Europe no more.

* The U. S. frigate " St. Lawrence."

From Mississippi and from Nile—
  From Baltic, Ganges, Bosphorus,
  In England's ark assembled thus
          Are friend and guest.
Look down the mighty sunlit aisle,
  And see the sumptuous banquet set,
  The brotherhood of nations met
          Around the feast !

Along the dazzling colonnade,
  Far as the straining eye can gaze,
  Gleam cross and fountain, bell and vase,
          In vistas bright ;
And statues fair of nymph and maid,
  And steeds and pards and Amazons,
  Writhing and grappling in the bronze,
          In endless fight.

          ۱

To deck the glorious roof and dome,
  To make the Queen a canopy,
  The peaceful hosts of industry
          Their standards bear.
Yon are the works of Brahmin loom ;
  On such a web of Persian thread
  The desert Arab bows his head
          And cries his prayer.

Look yonder where the engines toil :
  These England's arms of conquest are,
  The trophies of her bloodless war :
          Brave weapons these.
Victorious over wave and soil,
  With these she sails, she weaves, she tills
  Pierces the everlasting hills
          And spans the seas.

The engine roars upon its race,
  The shuttle whirrs along the woof,
  The people hum from floor to roof,
          With Babel tongue.
The fountain in the basin plays,
  The chanting organ echoes clear,
  An awful chorus 'tis to hear,
          A wondrous song !

Swell, organ, swell your trumpet blast,
  March, Queen and Royal pageant, march
  By splendid aisle and springing arch
          Of this fair Hall :
And see ! above the fabric vast,
  God's boundless heaven is bending blue,
  God's peaceful sunlight's beaming through.
          And shines o'er all.

May, 1851.

THE BALLAD OF BOUILLABAISSE.

A STREET there is in Paris famous,
  For which no rhyme our language yields,
Rue Neuve des Petits Champs its name is—
  The New Street of the little Fields.
And here's an inn, not rich and splendid,
  But still in comfortable case ;
The which in youth I oft attended,
  To eat a bowl of Bouillabaisse.

This Bouillabaisse a noble dish is—
  A sort of soup or broth, or brew,
Or hotchpotch of all sorts of fishes,
  That Greenwich never could outdo ;

Green herbs, red peppers, mussels, saffron,
　　Soles, onions, garlic, roach, and dace :
All these you eat at TERRÉ's tavern,
　　In that one dish of Bouillabaisse.

Indeed, a rich and savory stew 'tis ;
　　And true philosophers, methinks,
Who love all sorts of natural beauties,
　　Should love good victuals and good drinks.
And Cordelier or Benedictine
　　Might gladly, sure, his lot embrace,
Nor find a fast-day too afflicting,
　　Which served him up a Bouillabaisse.

I wonder if the house still there is ?
　　Yes, here the lamp is, as before ;
The smiling red-cheeked *écaillère* is
　　Still opening oysters at the door.
Is TERRÉ still alive and able ?
　　I recollect his droll grimace :
He'd come and smile before your table,
　　And hope you liked your Bouillabaisse.

We enter—nothing's changed or older.
　　" How's Monsieur TERRÉ, waiter, pray ?"
The waiter stares and shrugs his shoulder—
　　" Monsieur is dead this many a day."
" It is the lot of saint and sinner,
　　So honest TERRÉ's run his race."
" What will Monsieur require for dinner ?"
　　" Say, do you still cook Bouillabaisse ?"

"Oh, oui, Monsieur," 's the waiter's answer ;
　　" Quel vin Monsieur désire-t-il ?"
" Tell me a good one."—" That I can, Sir :
　　The Chambertin with yellow seal."

" So TERRÉ's gone," I say, and sink in
   My old accustom'd corner-place ;
" He's done with feasting and with drinking,
   With Burgundy and Bouillabaisse."

My old accustom'd corner here is,
   The table still is in the nook ;
Ah ! vanish'd many a busy year is
   This well-known chair since last I took.
When first I saw ye, *cari luoghi*,
   I'd scarce a beard upon my face,
And now a grizzled, grim old fogy,
   I sit and wait for Bouillabaisse.

Where are you, old companions trusty
   Of early days here met to dine ?
Come, waiter ! quick, a flagon crusty—
   I'll pledge them in the good old wine.
The kind old voices and old faces
   My memory can quick retrace ;
Around the board they take their places,
   And share the wine and Bouillabaisse.

There's JACK has made a wondrous marriage ;
   There's laughing TOM is laughing yet ;
There's brave AUGUSTUS drives his carriage ;
   There's poor old FRED in the *Gazette ;*
On JAMES's head the grass is growing :
   Good Lord ! the world has wagged apace
Since here we set the claret flowing,
   And drank, and ate the Bouillabaisse.

Ah me ! how quick the days are flitting !
   I mind me of a time that's gone,
When here I'd sit, as now I'm sitting,
   In this same place—but not alone.

A fair young form was nestled near me,
  A dear, dear face looked fondly up,
And sweetly spoke and smiled to cheer me
  —There's no one now to share my cup.

       *   *   *   *   *

I drink it as the Fates ordain it.
  Come, fill it, and have done with rhymes:
Fill up the lonely glass, and drain it
  In memory of dear old times.
Welcome the wine, whate'er the seal is;
  And sit you down and say your grace
With thankful heart, whate'er the meal is.
  —Here comes the smoking Bouillabaisse!

THE MAHOGANY TREE.

CHRISTMAS is here:
Winds whistle shrill,
Icy and chill,
Little care we:
Little we fear
Weather without,
Shelter about
The Mahogany Tree.

Once on the boughs
Birds of rare plume
Sang, in its bloom;
Night-birds are we:
Here we carouse,
Singing like them,
Perched round the stem
Of the jolly old tree.

Here let us sport,
Boys, as we sit ;
Laughter and wit
Flashing so free.
Life is but short—
When we are gone,
Let them sing on
Round the old tree.

Evenings we knew,
Happy as this ;
Faces we miss,
Pleasant to see.
Kind hearts and true,
Gentle and just,
Peace to your dust !
We sing round the tree.

Care, like a dun,
Lurks at the gate :
Let the dog wait ;
Happy we'll be !
Drink, every one ;
Pile up the coals,
Fill the red bowls,
Round the old tree !

Drain we the cup.—
Friend, art afraid ?
Spirits are laid
In the Red Sea.
Mantle it up ;
Empty it yet ;
Let us forget,
Round the old tree.

Sorrows, begone !
Life and its ills,

Duns and their bills,
Bid we to flee.
Come with the dawn,
Blue-devil sprite,
Leave us to-night,
Round the old tree.

THE YANKEE VOLUNTEERS.

"A surgeon of the United States Army says, that on
inquiring of the captain of his company, he found that
nine tenths of the men had enlisted on account of some
female difficulty."—*Morning Paper.*

Ye Yankee volunteers !
It makes my bosom bleed
When I your story read,
 Though oft 'tis told one.
So—in both hemispheres
The women are untrue,
And cruel in the New,
 As in the Old one !

What—in this company
Of sixty sons of Mars,
Who march'd neath Stripes and Stars,
 With fife and horn,
Nine tenths of all we see
Along the warlike line
Had but one cause to join
 This Hope Forlorn ?

Deserted from the realm
Where tyrant Venus reigns,
You slipp'd her wicked chains,
 Fled and outran her.

And now, with sword and helm,
Together banded are
Beneath the Stripe and Star-
    Embroider'd banner !

And is it so with all
The warriors ranged in line,
With lace bedizen'd fine
    And swords gold-hilted ?
Yon lusty corporal,
Yon color-man who gripes
The flag of Stars and Stripes—
    Has each been jilted ?

Come, each man of this line,
The privates strong and tall,
" The pioneers and all,"
    The fifer nimble—
Lieutenant and Ensign,
Captain with epaulets,
And Blacky there, who beats
    The clanging cymbal—

O cymbal-beating black,
Tell us, as thou canst feel,
Was it some Lucy Neal
    Who caused thy ruin ?
O nimble fifing Jack,
And drummer making din
So deftly on the skin,
    With thy rat-tattooing—

Confess, ye volunteers,
Lieutenant and Ensign,
And Captain of the line,
    As bold as Roman—

Confess, ye grenadiers,
However strong and tall,
The Conqueror of you all
        Is Woman, Woman !

No corselet is so proof
But through it from her bow
The shafts that she can throw
        Will pierce and rankle.
No champion e'er so tough,
But's in the struggle thrown,
And tripp'd and trodden down
        By her slim ankle.

Thus always it was ruled :
And when a woman smiled,
The strong man was a child,
        The sage a noodle.
Alcides was befool'd,
And silly Samson shorn,
Long, long ere you were born,
        Poor Yankee Doodle !

———

THE PEN AND THE ALBUM.

" I AM Miss Catherine's book," the Album
    speaks ;
" I've lain among your tomes these many weeks ;
I'm tired of their old coats and yellow cheeks.

" Quick, Pen ! and write a line with a good grace :
Come ! draw me off a funny little face ;
And, prithee, send me back to Chesham Place."

PEN.

"I am my master's faithful old Gold Pen ;
I've served him three long years, and drawn since
    then
Thousands of funny women and droll men.

"O Album ! could I tell you all his ways
And thoughts, since I am his, these thousand
    days,
Lord, how your pretty pages I'd amaze !"

ALBUM.

" His ways ? his thoughts ? Just whisper me a
    few ;
Tell me a curious anecdote or two,
And write 'em quickly off, good Mordan, do !"

PEN.

" Since he my faithful service did engage
To follow him through his queer pilgrimage
I've drawn and written many a line and page.

"Caricatures I scribbled have, and rhymes,
And dinner-cards, and picture pantomimes,
And merry little children's books at times.

" I've writ the foolish fancy of his brain ;
The aimless jest that, striking, hath caused pain ;
The idle word that he'd wish back again.

    *   *   *   *   *

" I've help'd him to pen many a line for bread ;
To joke, with sorrow aching in his head ;
And make your laughter when his own heart
    bled.

" I've spoke with men of all degree and sort—
Peers of the land, and ladies of the Court ;
Oh, but I've chronicled a deal of sport !

" Feasts that were ate a thousand days ago,
Biddings to wine that long hath ceased to flow,
Gay meetings with good fellows long laid low ;

" Summons to bridal, banquet, burial, ball,
Tradesmen's polite reminders of his small
Account due Christmas last—I've answer'd all.

" Poor Diddler's tenth petition for a half-
Guinea ; Miss Bunyan's for an autograph ;
So I refuse, accept, lament, or laugh,

" Condole, congratulate, invite, praise, scoff,
Day after day still dipping in my trough,
And scribbling pages after pages off.

" Day after day the labor's to be done,
And sure as come the postman and the sun,
The indefatigable ink must run.

*　　*　　*　　*　　*

" Go back, my pretty little gilded tome,
To a fair mistress and a pleasant home,
Where soft hearts greet us whensoe'er we come !

" Dear, friendly eyes, with constant kindness lit,
However rude my verse, or poor my wit,
Or sad or gay my mood, you welcome it.

" Kind lady ! till my last of lines is penn'd,
My master's love, grief, laughter, at an end,
Whene'er I write your name, may I write friend !

" Not all are so that were so in past years ;
Voices, familiar once, no more he hears ;
Names, often writ, are blotted out in tears.

"So be it :—joys will end and tears will dry—
Album ! my master bids me wish good-by
He'll send you to your mistress presently.

" And thus with thankful heart he closes you :
Blessing the happy hour when a friend he knew
So gentle, and so generous, and so true.

" Nor pass the words as idle phrases by ;
Stranger ! I never writ a flattery,
Nor sign'd the page that register'd a lie."

———

MRS. KATHERINE'S LANTERN.

WRITTEN IN A LADY'S ALBUM.

" Coming from a gloomy court,
Place of Israelite resort,
This old lamp I've brought with me.
Madam, on its panes you'll see
The initials K and E."

" An old lantern brought to me ?
Ugly, dingy, battered, black !"
(Here a lady I suppose
Turning up a pretty nose)—
" Pray, sir, take the old thing back.
I've no taste for *bric-à-brac.*"

" Please to mark the letters twain"—
(I'm supposed to speak again)—

"Graven on the lantern pane.
Can you tell me who was she,
Mistress of the flowery wreath,
And the anagram beneath—
The mysterious K E ?

" Full a hundred years are gone
Since the little beacon shone
From a Venice balcony :
There, on summer nights, it hung,
And her lovers came and sung
To their beautiful K E.

" Hush ! in the canal below
Don't you hear the plash of oars
Underneath the lantern's glow,
And a thrilling voice begins
To the sound of mandolins ?—
Begins singing of amore
And delire and dolore—
O the ravishing tenore !

" Lady, do you know the tune ?
Ah, we all of us have hummed it !
I've an old guitar has thrummed it,
Under many a changing moon.
Shall I try it ? *Do* RE MI * *
What is this ? *Ma foi*, the fact is,
That my hand is out of practice,
And my poor old fiddle cracked is,
And a man—I let the truth out—
Who's had almost every tooth out,
Cannot sing as once he sung,
When he was young as you are young,
When he was young and lutes were strung,
And love-lamps in the casement hung."

LUCY'S BIRTHDAY.

SEVENTEEN rose-buds in a ring,
   Thick with sister flowers beset,
   In a fragrant coronet,
Lucy's servants this day bring.
   Be it the birthday wreath she wears
Fresh and fair, and symbolling
   The young number of her years,
The sweet blushes of her spring.

Types of youth and love and hope !
   Friendly hearts your mistress greet,
   Be you ever fair and sweet,
And grow lovelier as you ope !
   Gentle nurseling, fenced about
With fond care, and guarded so,
   Scarce you've heard of storms without,
Frosts that bite, or winds that blow !

Kindly has your life begun,
   And we pray that Heaven may send
To our floweret a warm sun,
   A calm summer, a sweet end.
And where'er shall be her home,
   May she decorate the place ;
Still expanding into bloom,
   And developing in grace.

THE CANE-BOTTOM'D CHAIR.

IN tattered old slippers that toast at the bars,
And a ragged old jacket perfumed with cigars,
Away from the world and its toils and its cares,
I've a snug little kingdom up four pair of stairs.

To mount to this realm is a toil, to be sure,
But the fire there is bright and the air rather
    pure ;
And the view I behold on a sunshiny day
Is grand through the chimney-pots over the way.

This snug little chamber is cramm'd in all nooks
With worthless old knicknacks and silly old books,
And foolish old odds and foolish old ends,
Crack'd bargains from brokers, cheap keepsakes
    from friends.

Old armor, prints, pictures, pipes, china (all
    crack'd),
Old rickety tables, and chairs broken-backed ;
A twopenny treasury, wondrous to see ;
What matter ? 'tis pleasant to you, friend, and me.

No better divan need the Sultan require,
Than the creaking old sofa that basks by the fire ;
And 'tis wonderful, surely, what music you get
From the rickety, ramshackle, wheezy spinet.

That praying-rug came from a Turcoman's camp ;
By Tiber once twinkled that brazen old lamp ;
A Mameluke fierce yonder dagger has drawn :
'Tis a murderous knife to toast muffins upon.

Long, long through the hours, and the night, and
    the chimes,
Here we talk of old books, and old friends, and
    old times ;
As we sit in a fog made of rich Latakie
This chamber is pleasant to you, friend, and me.

But of all the cheap treasures that garnish my nest.
There's one that I love and I cherish the best :

For the finest of couches that's padded with hair
I never would change thee, my cane-bottom'd
   chair.

'Tis a bandy-legg'd, high-shoulder'd, worm-eaten
   seat,
With a creaking old back and twisted old feet ;
But since the fair morning when Fanny sat there,
I bless thee and love thee, old cane-bottom'd
   chair.

If chairs have but feeling, in holding such
   charms
A thrill must have pass'd through your wither'd
   old arms !
I look'd, and I long'd, and I wish'd in despair ;
I wished myself turn'd to a cane-bottom'd chair.

It was but a moment she sat in this place,
She'd a scarf on her neck, and a smile on her
   face !
A smile on her face, and a rose in her hair,
And she sat there, and bloom'd in my cane-
   bottom'd chair.

And so I have valued my chair ever since,
Like the shrine of a saint, or the throne of a
   prince ;
Saint Fanny, my patroness sweet I declare,
The queen of my heart and my cane-bottom'd
   chair.

When the candles burn low, and the company's
   gone,
In the silence of night as I sit here alone—
I sit here alone, but we yet are a pair—
My Fanny I see in my cane-bottom'd chair.

She comes from the past and revisits my room ;
She looks as she then did, all beauty and bloom :
So smiling and tender, so fresh and so fair,
And yonder she sits in my cane-bottom'd chair.

PISCATOR AND PISCATRIX.

LINES WRITTEN TO AN ALBUM PRINT.

As on this pictured page I look,
This pretty tale of line and hook
As though it were a novel-book
    Amuses and engages :
I know them both, the boy and girl ;
She is the daughter of the Earl,
The lad (that has his hair in curl)
    My lord the County's page is.

A pleasant place for such a pair !
The fields lie basking in the glare ;
No breath of wind the heavy air
    Of lazy summer quickens.
Hard by you see the castle tall ;
The village nestles round the wall,
As round about the hen its small
    Young progeny of chickens.

It is too hot to pace the keep ;
To climb the turret is too steep ;
My lord the Earl is dozing deep,
    His noonday dinner over :
The postern-warder is asleep
(Perhaps they've bribed him not to peep) :
And so from out the gate they creep,
    And cross the fields of clover.

Their lines into the brook they launch ;
He lays his cloak upon a branch,
To guarantee his Lady Blanche
    's delicate complexion :
He takes his rapier from his haunch,
That beardless doughty champion staunch }
He'd drill it through the rival's paunch
    That question'd his affection !

O heedless pair of sportsmen slack !
You never mark, though trout or jack,
Or little foolish stickleback,
    Your baited snares may capture.
What care has *she* for line and hook ?
She turns her back upon the brook,
Upon her lover's eyes to look
    In sentimental rapture.

O loving pair ! as thus I gaze
Upon the girl who smiles always,
The little hand that ever plays
    Upon the lover's shoulder ;
In looking at your pretty shapes,
A sort of envious wish escapes
(Such as the Fox had for the Grapes)
    The Poet your beholder.

To be brave, handsome, twenty-two ,
With nothing else on earth to do,
But all day long to bill and coo :
    It were a pleasant calling.
And had I such a partner sweet ;
A tender heart for mine to beat,
A gentle hand my clasp to meet ;—
    I'd let the world flow at my feet,
    And never heed its brawling.

THE ROSE UPON MY BALCONY,

THE rose upon my balcony the morning air per
    fuming,
  Was leafless all the winter time and pining for
    the spring ;
You ask me why her breath is sweet, and why
    her cheek is blooming :
  It is because the sun is out and birds begin to
    sing.

The nightingale, whose melody is through the
    greenwood ringing,
  Was silent when the boughs were bare and
    winds were blowing keen :
And if, Mamma, you ask of me the reason of his
    singing,
  It is because the sun is out and all the leaves
    are green.

Thus each performs his part, Mamma : the birds
    have found their voices,
  The blowing rose a flush, Mamma, her bonny
    cheek to dye ;
And there's sunshine in my heart, Mamma, which
    wakens and rejoices,
  And so I sing and blush, Mamma, and that's
    the reason why.

RONSARD TO HIS MISTRESS.

"Quand vous serez bien vieille, au soir à la chandelle,
Assise auprès du feu devisant et filant,
Direz, chantant mes vers en vous esmerveillant :
Ronsard me célébroit du temps que j'étois belle."

SOME winter night, shut snugly in
  Beside the fagot in the hall,
I think I see you sit and spin,
  Surrounded by your maidens all.
Old tales are told, old songs are sung,
  Old days come back to memory ;
You say, " When I was fair and young,
  A poet sang of me !"

There's not a maiden in your hall,
  Though tired and sleepy ever so,
But wakes, as you my name recall,
  And longs the history to know.
And, as the piteous tale is said,
  Of lady cold and lover true,
Each, musing, carries it to bed,
  And sighs and envies you !

" Our lady's old and feeble now,"
  They'll say ; " she once was fresh and fair,
And yet she spurn'd her lover's vow,
  And heartless left him to despair :
The lover lies in silent earth,
  No kindly mate the lady cheers :
She sits beside a lonely hearth,
  With threescore and ten years !"

Ah ! dreary thoughts and dreams are those,
  But wherefore yield me to despair,

While yet the poet's bosom glows,
    While yet the dame is peerless fair ?
Sweet lady mine ! while yet 'tis time
    Requite my passion and my truth,
And gather in their blushing prime
    The roses of your youth !

AT THE CHURCH GATE.

ALTHOUGH I enter not,
Yet round about the spot
    Ofttimes I hover :
And near the sacred gate,
With longing eyes I wait,
    Expectant of her.

The Minster bell tolls out
Above the city's rout,
    And noise and humming :
They've hushed the Minster bell :
The organ 'gins to swell :
    She's coming, she's coming !

My lady comes at last,
Timid, and stepping fast,
    And hastening hither,
With modest eyes downcast :
She comes—she's here—she's past—
    May Heaven go with her !

Kneel, undisturb'd, fair Saint !
Pour out your praise or plaint
    Meekly and duly ;

I will not enter there,
To sully your pure prayer
    With thoughts unruly.

But suffer me to pace
Round the forbidden place,
    Lingering a minute
Like outcast spirits who wait
And see through heaven's gate
    Angels within it.

———

THE AGE OF WISDOM.

Ho, pretty page, with the dimpled chin,
    That never has known the barber's shear,
All your wish is woman to win,
This is the way that boys begin,—
    Wait till you come to Forty Year.

Curly gold locks cover foolish brains,
    Billing and cooing is all your cheer ;
Sighing and singing of midnight strains,
Under Bonnybell's window panes,—
    Wait till you come to Forty Year.

Forty times over let Michaelmas pass,
    Grizzling hair the brain doth clear—
Then you know a boy is an ass,
Then you know the worth of a lass,
    Once you have come to Forty Year.

Pledge me round, I bid ye declare,
    All good fellows whose beards are gray

Did not the fairest of the fair
Common grow and wearisome ere
   Ever a month was pass'd away?

The reddest lips that ever have kissed,
   The brightest eyes that ever have shone,
May pray and whisper, and we not list,
Or look away, and never be missed,
   Ere yet ever a month is gone.

Gillian's dead, God rest her bier,
   How I loved her twenty years syne!
Marian's married, but I sit here
Alone and merry at Forty Year,
   Dipping my nose in the Gascon wine.

SORROWS OF WERTHER.

WERTHER had a love for Charlotte
   Such as words could never utter;
Would you know how first he met her?
   She was cutting bread and butter.

Charlotte was a married lady,
   And a moral man was Werther,
And, for all the wealth of Indies,
   Would do nothing for to hurt her.

So he sighed and pined and ogled,
   And his passion boiled and bubbled,
Till he blew his silly brains out,
   And no more was by it troubled.

Charlotte, having seen his body
  Borne before her on a shutter,
Like a well-conducted person,
  Went on cutting bread and butter.

———

A DOE IN THE CITY.

LITTLE KITTY LORIMER,
  Fair, and young, and witty,
What has brought your ladyship
  Rambling to the City?

All the Stags in Capel Court
  Saw her lightly trip it ;
All the lads of Stock Exchange
  Twigg'd her muff and tippet.

With a sweet perplexity,
  And a mystery pretty,
Threading through Threadneedle Street,
  Trots the little KITTY.

What was my astonishment—
  What was my compunction,
When she reached the Offices
  Of the Didland Junction !

Up the Didland stairs she went,
  To the Didland door, Sir ;
Porters, lost in wonderment,
  Let her pass before, Sir.

" Madam," says the old chief Clerk,
  " Sure we can't admit ye."

" Where's the Didland Junction deed ?"
Dauntlessly says KITTY.

" If you doubt my honesty,
Look at my receipt, Sir."
Up then jumps the old chief Clerk,
Smiling as he meets her.

KITTY at the table sits
(Whither the old Clerk leads her),
" *I deliver this*," she says,
" *As my act and deed, Sir.*"

When I heard these funny words
Come from lips so pretty,
This, I thought, should surely be
Subject for a ditty.

What ! are ladies stagging it ?
Sure, the more's the pity ;
But I've lost my heart to her,—
Naughty little KITTY.

THE LAST OF MAY.

(IN REPLY TO AN INVITATION DATED ON THE 1ST.)

By fate's benevolant award,
Should I survive the day,
I'll drink a bumper with my lord
Upon the last of May.

That I may reach that happy time
The kindly gods I pray,

For are not ducks and peas in prime
    Upon the last of May?

At thirty boards, 'twixt now and then,
    My knife and fork shall play;
But better wine and better men
    I shall not meet in May.

And though, good friend, with whom I dine,
    Your honest head is gray,
And, like this grizzled head of mine,
    Has seen its last of May;

Yet, with a heart that's ever kind,
    A gentle spirit gay,
You've spring perennial in your mind,
    And round you make a May!

———

"AH, BLEAK AND BARREN WAS THE MOOR."

Ah! bleak and barren was the moor,
    Ah! loud and piercing was the storm,
The cottage roof was sheltered sure,
    The cottage hearth was bright and warm—
An orphan-boy the lattice pass'd,
    And, as he marked its cheerful glow,
Felt doubly keen the midnight blast,
    And doubly cold the fallen snow.

They marked him as he onward press'd,
    With fainting heart and weary limb;
Kind voices bade him turn and rest,
    And gentle faces welcomed him.

The dawn is up—the guest is gone,
　The cottage hearth is blazing still :
Heaven pity all poor wanderers lone !
　Hark to the wind upon the hill !

———

SONG OF THE VIOLET.

A HUMBLE flower long time I pined
　Upon the solitary plain,
And trembled at the angry wind,
　And shrunk before the bitter rain.
And oh ! 'twas in a blessed hour
　A passing wanderer chanced to see,
And, pitying the lonely flower,
　To stoop and gather me.

I fear no more the tempest rude,
　On dreary heath no more I pine,
But left my cheerless solitude,
　To deck the breast of Caroline.
Alas ! our days are brief at best,
　Nor long, I fear, will mine endure,
Though sheltered here upon a breast
　So gentle and so pure.

It draws the fragrance from my leaves
　It robs me of my sweetest breath,
And every time it falls and heaves,
　It warns me of my coming death.
But one I know would glad forego
　All joys of life to be as I ;
An hour to rest on that sweet breast,
　And then, contented, die.

FAIRY DAYS.

BESIDE the old hall-fire—upon my nurse's knee,
Of happy fairy days—what tales were told to me !
I thought the world was once—all peopled with
    princesses,
And my heart would beat to hear—their loves and
    their distresses ;
And many a quiet night,—in slumber sweet and
    deep,
The pretty fairy people—would visit me in sleep.

I saw them in my dreams—come flying east and
    west,
With wondrous fairy gifts—the new-born babe
    they bless'd ;
One has brought a jewel—and one a crown of gold,
And one has brought a curse—but she is wrinkled
    and old.
The gentle queen turns pale—to hear those words
    of sin,
But the king he only laughs—and bids the dance
    begin.

The babe has grown to be—the fairest of the land,
And rides the forest green—a hawk upon her
    hand,
An ambling palfrey white—a golden robe and
    crown :
I've seen her in my dreams—riding up and down :
And heard the ogre laugh—as she fell into his
    snare,
At the little tender creature—who wept and tore
    her hair !

But ever when it seemed—her need was at the
 sorest,
A prince in shining mail—comes prancing through
 the forest,
A waving ostrich-plume—a buckler burnished
 bright ;
I've seen him in my dreams—good sooth ! a
 gallant knight.
His lips are coral red—beneath a dark mustache ;
See how he waves his hand—and how his blue
 eyes flash !

" Come forth, thou Paynim knight !"—he shouts
 in accents clear.
The giant and the maid—both tremble his voice
 to hear.
Saint Mary guard him well !—he draws his
 falchion keen,
The giant and the knight—are fighting on the
 green.
I see them in my dreams—his blade gives stroke
 on stroke,
The giant pants and reels—and tumbles like an
 oak !

With what a blushing grace—he falls upon his
 knee
And takes the lady's hand— and whispers, " You
 are free !"
Ah ! happy childish tales—of knight and faërie !
I waken from my dreams—but there's ne'er a
 knight for me ;
I waken from my dreams—and wish that I could
 be
A child by the old hall-fire—upon my nurse's
 knee !

POCAHONTAS.

WEARIED arm and broken sword
　Wage in vain the desperate fight :
Round him press a countless horde,
　He is but a single knight.
Hark ! a cry of triumph shrill
　Through the wilderness resounds,
　As, with twenty bleeding wounds,
Sinks the warrior, fighting still.

Now they heap the fatal pyre,
　And the torch of death they light ;
Ah ! 'tis hard to die of fire !
　Who will shield the captive knight ?
Round the stake with fiendish cry
　Wheel and dance the savage crowd,
　Cold the victim's mien, and proud,
And his breast is bared to die.

Who will shield the fearless heart ?
　Who avert the murderous blade ?
From the throng, with sudden start,
　See there springs an Indian maid.
Quick she stands before the knight :
　" Loose the chain, unbind the ring ;
　I am daughter of the king,
And I claim the Indian right !"

Dauntlessly aside she flings
　Lifted axe and thirsty knife ;
Fondly to his heart she clings,
　And her bosom guards his life !
In the woods of Powhattan,
　Still 'tis told by Indian fires,
　How a daughter of their sires
Saved the captive Englishman.

FROM POCAHONTAS.

RETURNING from the cruel fight
How pale and faint appears my knight !
He sees me anxious at his side ;
" Why seek, my love, your wounds to hide?
Or deem your English girl afraid
To emulate the Indian maid?"

Be mine my husband's grief to cheer,
In peril to be ever near ;
Whate'er of ill or woe betide,
To bear it clinging at his side ;
The poisoned stroke of fate to ward,
His bosom with my own to guard :
Ah ! could it spare a pang to his,
It could not know a purer bliss !
'Twould gladden as it felt the smart,
And thank the hand that flung the dart !

———

THE LEGEND OF ST. SOPHIA OF KIOFF.

AN EPIC POEM, IN TWENTY BOOKS.

I.

[The poet describes the city and spelling of Kiow, Kioff,
or Kiova.]

A THOUSAND years ago, or more,
　A city filled with burghers stout,
　　And girt with ramparts round about,
Stood on the rocky Dnieper shore.

In armor bright, by day and night,
   The sentries they paced to and fro.
Well guarded and walled was this town, and
   called
   By different names, I'd have you to know ;
For if you looks in the g'ography books,
In those dictionaries the name it varies,
And they write it off Kieff or Kioff,
               Kiova or Kiow.

II.

[Its buildings, public works, and ordinances, religious
and civil.—The poet shows how a certain priest dwelt
at Kioff, a godly clergyman, and one that preached
rare good sermons.]

Thus guarded without by wall and redoubt,
   Kiova within was a place of renown,
With more advantages than in those dark ages
   Were commonly known to belong to a town.
There were places and squares, and each year
   four fairs,
And regular aldermen and regular lord mayors ;
And streets, and alleys, and a bishop's palace ;
And a church with clocks for the orthodox—
With clocks and with spires, as religion desires;
And beadles to whip the bad little boys
Over their poor little corduroys,
In service-time when they *didn't* make a noise ;
And a chapter and dean, and a cathedral-green
With ancient trees, underneath whose shades
Wandered nice young nursery-maids.
Ding-dong, ding-dong, ding-ding-a-ring-ding,
The bells they made a merry merry ring,
From the tall tall steeple ; and all the people
(Except the Jews) came and filled the pews—
     Poles, Russians and Germans,
      To hear the sermons

Which HYACINTH preached to those Germans
    and Poles
  For the safety of their souls.

III.

[How this priest was short and fat of body ;]

A worthy priest he was and a stout—
  You've seldom looked on such a one ;
For, though he fasted thrice in a week,
Yet nevertheless his skin was sleek ;
His waist it spanned two yards about,
  And he weighed a score of stone.

IV.

[And like unto the author of " Plymley's Letters."]

A worthy priest for fasting and prayer
  And mortification most deserving,
And as for preaching beyond compare :
He'd exert his powers for three or four hours
With greater pith than Sydney Smith
  Or the Reverend Edward Irving,

▼.

[Of what convent he was prior, and when the convent
  was built.]

He was the prior of Saint Sophia
(A Cockney rhyme, but no better I know)—
Of St. Sophia, that Church in Kiow,
  Built by missionaries I can't tell when ;
Who by their discussions converted the Russians
  And made them Christian men.

VI.

[Of Saint Sophia of Kioff ; and how her statue miracu-
lously travelled thither.]

Sainted Sophia (so the legend vows)
With special favor did regard this house ;
  And to uphold her converts' new devotion
Her statue (needing but her legs for *her* ship)
  Walks of itself across the German Ocean ;
        And of a sudden perches
        In this the best of churches,
Whither all Kiovites come and pay it grateful
  worship.

VII.

[And how Kioff should have been a happy city ; but that]

Thus with her patron-saints and pious preachers
  Recorded here in catalogue precise,
A goodly city, worthy magistrates,
You would have thought in all the Russian states
The citizens the happiest of all creatures,—
  The town itself a perfect Paradise.

VIII.

[Certain wicked Cossacks did besiege it, murdering the
citizens, until they agreed to pay a tribute yearly.—
How they paid the tribute, and then suddenly refused
it, to the wonder of the Cossack envoy.—Of a mighty
gallant speech that the lord-mayor made, exhorting
the burghers to pay no longer.]

No, alas ! this well-built city
  Was in a perpetual fidget ;
For the Tartars, without pity
  Did remorselessly besiege it.

Tartars fierce, with swords and sabres,
  Huns and Turks, and such as these,

Envied much their peaceful neighbors
　　By the blue Borysthenes.

Down they came, these ruthless Russians,
　　From their steppes, and woods, and fens,
For to levy contributions
　　On the peaceful citizens.

Winter, Summer, Spring, and Autumn,
　　Down they came to peaceful Kioff,
Killed the burghers when they caught 'em
　　If their lives they would not buy off.

Till the city, quite confounded
　　By the ravages they made,
Humbly with their chief compounded,
　　And a yearly tribute paid.

Which (because their courage lax was)
　　They discharged while they were able:
Tolerated thus the tax was,
　　Till it grew intolerable,

And the Calmuc envoy sent,
　　As before to take their dues all,
Got, to his astonishment,
　　A unanimous refusal!

" Men of Kioff!" thus courageous
　　Did the stout lord-mayor harangue them,
" Wherefore pay these sneaking wages
　　To the hectoring Russians? hang them!

" Hark!　I hear the awful cry of
　　Our forefathers in their graves;
" ' Fight, ye citizens of Kioff!
　　Kioff was not made for slaves.'

" All too long have ye betrayed her ;
  Rouse, ye men and aldermen,
Send the insolent invader—
  Send him starving back again."

IX.

[Of their thanks and heroic resolves.—They dismiss the
  envoy, and set about drilling.—Of the city guard :
  viz. militia, dragoons, and bombardiers, and their
  commanders.—Of the majors and captains, the fortifi-
  cations and artillery.—Of the conduct of the actors and
  the clergy.—Of the ladies ; and, finally, of the taylors.]

He spoke and he sat down ; the people of the
    town,
  Who were fired with a brave emulation,
Now rose with one accord, and voted thanks
    unto the lord-
  Mayor for his oration :

The envoy they dismissed, never placing in his
    fist
  So much as a single shilling ;
And all with courage fired, as his lordship he
    desired,
  At once set about their drilling.

Then every city ward established a guard,
    Diurnal and nocturnal :
Militia volunteers, light dragoons, and bombar-
    diers,
  With an alderman for colonel.

There was muster and roll-calls, and repairing
    city walls,
  And filling up of fosses :

And the captains and the majors, so gallant and
    courageous,
  A-riding about on their hosses.

To be guarded at all hours they built themselves
    watch-towers,
  With every tower a man on ;
And surely and secure, each from out his embra-
    sure,
  Looked down the iron cannon !

A battle-song was writ for the theatre, where it
    Was sung with vast enérgy
And rapturous applause ; and besides, the public
    cause
  Was supported by the clergy.

The pretty ladies'-maids were pinning of cock-
    ades,
  And tying on of sashes ;
And dropping gentle tears, while their lovers
    bluster'd fierce
  About gun-shot and gashes ;

The ladies took the hint, and all day were scrap-
    ing lint,
  As became their softer genders ;
And got bandages and beds for the limbs and for
    the heads
  Of the city's brave defenders.

The men, both young and old, felt resolute and
    bold,
  And panted hot for glory ;
Even the tailors 'gan to brag, and embroidered
    on their flag,
    " AUT WINCERE AUT MORI."

X.

[Of the Cossack chief—his stratagem ; and the burghers'
sillie victorie.—What prisoners they took, and how
conceited they were of the Cossack chief—his orders ;
and how he feigned a retreat.—The warder proclayms
the Cossacks' retreat, and the citie greatly rejoyces.]

Seeing the city's resolute condition,
   The Cossack chief, too cunning to despise it,
Said to himself, " Not having ammunition
Wherewith to batter the place in proper form,
Some of these nights I'll carry it by storm,
   And sudden escalade it or surprise it.

" Let's see, however, if the cits stand firmish."
   He rode up to the city gates ; for answers,
Out rushed an eager troop of the town *élite*,
And straightway did begin a gallant skirmish :
The Cossack hereupon did sound retreat,
   Leaving the victory with the city lancers.

They took two prisoners and as many horses,
   And the whole town grew quickly so elate
With this small victory of their virgin forces,
That they did deem their privates and command
    ers
So many Cæsars, Pompeys, Alexanders,
   Napoleons, or Fredericks the Great.

And puffing with inordinate conceit
   They utterly despised these Cossack thieves ;
And thought the ruffians easier to beat
Than porters carpets think, or ushers boys.
Meanwhile, a sly spectator of their joys,
   The Cossack captain giggled in his sleeves.

" Whene'er you meet yon stupid city hogs"
   (He bade his troops precise this order keep),

" Don't stand a moment—run away, you dogs !"
'Twas done ; and when they met the town bat-
    talions,
The Cossacks, as if frightened at their valiance,
    Turned tail, and bolted like so many sheep.

They fled, obedient to their captain's order :
    And now this bloodless siege a month had
        lasted,
When, viewing the country round, the city warder
    (Who, like a faithful weathercock, did perch
Upon the steeple of St. Sophy's church),
    Sudden his trumpet took, and a mighty blast
    he blasted.

His voice it might be heard through all the streets
    (He was a warder wondrous strong in lung),
" Victory, victory ! the foe retreats !"
" The foe retreats !" each cries to each he meets ;
" The foe retreats !" each in his turn repeats.
Gods ! how the guns did roar, and how the joy-
    bells rung !

Arming in haste his gallant city lancers,
    The mayor, to learn if true the news might be,
A league or two out issued with his prancers.
    The Cossacks (something had given their cour-
        age a damper)
Hastened their flight, and 'gan like mad to scam-
    per ;
    Blessed be all the saints, Kiova town was free !

XI.

[The manner of the citic's rejoycings, and its impiety.—
    How the priest, Hyacinth, waited at church, and
    nobody came thither.]

Now, puffed with pride, the mayor grew vain,
Fought all his battles o'er again ;

And thrice he routed all his foes, and thrice he
    slew the slain.
'Tis true he might amuse himself thus,
And not be very murderous ;
For as of those who to death were done
The number was exactly *none*,
His lordship, in his soul's elation,
Did take a bloodless recreation—
Going home again, he did ordain
A very splendid cold collation
For the magistrates and the corporation ;
Likewise a grand illumination
For the amusement of the nation.
That night the theatres were free,
The conduits they ran Malvoisie ;
Each house that night did beam with light
And sound with mirth and jollity :
But shame, O shame ! not a soul in the town,
Now the city was safe and the Cossacks flown,
Ever thought of the bountiful saint by whose
    care
    The town had been rid of these terrible Turks—
Said even a prayer to that patroness fair
    For these her wondrous works !
Lord Hyacinth waited, the meekest of priors—
He waited at church with the rest of his friars ;
He went there at noon and he waited till ten,
Expecting in vain the lord-mayor and his men.
    He waited and waited from mid-day to dark ;
But in vain—you might search through the whole
    of the church,
Not a layman, alas ! to the city's disgrace,
From mid-day to dark showed his nose in the
    place.
    The pew-woman, organist, beadle, and clerk,
Kept away from their work, and were dancing
    like mad

Away in the streets with the other mad people,
Not thinking to pray, but to guzzle and tipple
Wherever the drink might be had.

XII.

[How he went forth to bid them to prayer.—How the
grooms and lackeys jeered him.—And the mayor,
mayoress, and aldermen, being tipsie, refused to go to
church.]

Amidst this din and revelry throughout the city
    roaring,
The silver moon rose silently, and high in heaven
    soaring ;
Prior Hyacinth was fervently upon his knees
    adoring :
" Toward my precious patroness this conduct
    sure unfair is ;
I cannot think, I must confess, what keeps the
    dignitaries
And our good mayor away, unless some business
    them contraries."

He puts his long white mantle on, and forth the
    prior sallies—
(His pious thoughts were bent upon good deeds
    and not on malice):
Heavens ! how the banquet lights they shone
    about the mayor's palace !
About the hall the scullions ran with meats both
    fresh and potted ;
The pages came with cup and can, all for the
    guests allotted ;
Ah, how they jeered that good fat man as up the
    stairs he trotted !

He entered in the ante-rooms where sat the may-
    or's court in ;

He found a pack of drunken grooms a-dicing and
a-sporting ;
The horrid wine and 'bacco fumes, they set the
prior a-snorting !
The prior thought he'd speak about their sins
before he went hence,
And lustily began to shout of sin and of repent-
ance ;
The rogues, they kicked the prior out before he'd
done a sentence !

And having got no portion small of buffeting
and tussling,
At last he reached the banquet-hall, where sat
the mayor a-guzzling,
And by his side his lady tall dressed out in white
sprig muslin.
Around the table in a ring the guests were drinking heavy ;
They drunk the church, and drunk the king, and
the army and the navy ;
In fact they'd toasted everything.   The prior
said, " God save ye !"

The mayor cried, " Bring a silver cup—there's
one upon the buffet ;
And, Prior, have the venison up—it's capital
réchauffé.
And so, Sir Priest, you've come to sup?   And
pray you, how's Saint Sophy ?"
The prior's face quite red was grown with horror
and with anger ;
He flung the proffered goblet down—it made a
hideous clangor ;
And 'gan a-preaching with a frown—he was a
fierce haranguer.

He tried the mayor and aldermen—they all set up
     a-jeering :
He tried the common-councilmen—they too be-
     gan a-sneering :
He turned toward the may'ress then, and hoped
     to get a hearing.
He knelt and seized her dinner-dress, made of the
     muslin snowy,
" To church, to church, my sweet mistress !"
     he cried ; " the way I'll show ye."
Alas, the lady-mayoress fell back as drunk as
     Chloe !

XIII.

[How the prior went back alone, and shut him.elf into
     Saint Sophia's chapel with his brethren.]

Out from this dissolute and drunken court
     Went the good prior, his eyes with weeping
       dim :
He tried the people of a meaner sort—
They too, alas, were bent upon their sport,
     And not a single soul would follow him !
But all were swigging schnapps and guzzling
     beer.

He found the cits, their daughters, sons, and
     spouses,
Spending the live-long night in fierce carouses :
     Alas, unthinking of the danger near !
One or two sentinels the ramparts guarded,
     The rest were sharing in the general feast :
" God wot, our tipsy town is poorly warded ;
     Sweet Saint Sophia help us !" cried the priest.

Alone he entered the cathedral gate,
     Careful he locked the mighty oaken door :

Within his company of monks did wait,
  A dozen poor old pious men—no more.
  Oh, but it grieved the gentle prior sore,
To think of those lost souls, given up to drink
    and fate !

The mighty outer gate well barred and fast,
  The poor old friars stirred their poor old bones,
  And pattering swiftly on the damp cold stones,
They through the solitary chancel passed.
The chancel walls looked black and dim and vast,
  And rendered, ghost-like, melancholy tones.

Onward the fathers sped, till coming nigh a
  Small iron gate, the which they entered quick at,
  They locked and double-locked the inner wicket
And stood within the chapel of Sophia.
Vain were it to describe this sainted place,
  Vain to describe that celebrated trophy,
  The venerable statue of Saint Sophy,
Which formed its chiefest ornament and grace.

Here the good prior, his personal griefs and
    sorrows
  In his extreme devotion quickly merging,
At once began to pray with voice sonorous ;
The other friars joined in pious chorus,
  And passed the night in singing, praying,
    scourging,
  In honor of Sophia, that sweet virgin.

XIV.

[The episode of Sneezoff and Katinka.—How the sentrie
  Sneezoff was surprised and slayn.]

    Leaving thus the pious priest in
      Humble penitence and prayer.

And the greedy cits a-feasting,
  Let us to the walls repair.

Walking by the sentry-boxes,
  Underneath the silver moon,
Lo ! the sentry boldly cocks his—
  Boldly cocks his musketoon.

Sneezoff was his designation.
  Fair-haired boy, forever pitied ;
For to take his cruel station,
  He but now Katinka quitted.

Poor in purse were both, but rich in
  Tender love's delicious plenties ;
She a damsel of the kitchen,
  He a haberdasher's 'prentice.

'Tinka, maiden tender-hearted,
  Was dissolved in tearful fits,
On that fatal night she parted
  From her darling, fair-haired Fritz.

Warm her soldier lad she wrapt in
  Comforter and muffettee ;
Called him "general" and "captain,"
  Though a simple private he.

"On your bosom wear this plaster,
  'Twill defend you from the cold ;
In your pipe smoke this canaster—
  Smuggled 'tis, my love, and old.

"All the night, my love, I'll miss you."
  Thus she spoke ; and from the door
Fair-haired Sneezoff made his issue,
  To return, alas, no more.

He it is who calmly walks his
    Walk beneath the silver moon ;
He it is who boldly cocks his
    Detonating musketoon.

He the bland canaster puffing,
    As upon his round he paces,
Sudden sees a ragamuffin
    Clambering swiftly up the glacis.

" Who goes there ?" exclaims the sentry ;
    " When the sun has once gone down
No one ever makes an entry
    Into this here fortified town !"

Shouted thus the watchful Sneezoff ;
    But, ere any one replied,
Wretched youth ! he fired his piece off,
    Started, staggered, groaned, and died !

XV.

[How the Cossacks rushed in suddenly and took the citie.
    —Of the Cossack troops, and of their manner of
    burning, murdering, and ravishing.—How they burned
    the whole citie down, save the church, whereof the
    bells began to ring.]

Ah, full well might the sentinel cry, " Who goes
    there ?"
But echo was frightened too much to declare.
Who goes there ? who goes there ? Can any one
    swear
To the number of sands *sur les bords de la mer*,
Or the whiskers of D'Orsay count down to a hair ?
As well might you tell of the sands the amount,
Or number each hair in each curl of the Count,
As ever proclaim the number and name

Of the hundreds and thousands that up the wal
    came !
Down, down the knaves poured with fire and with
    sword :
There were thieves from the Danube and rogues
    from the Don ;
There were Turks and Wallacks, and shouting
    Cossacks ;
Of all nations and regions, and tongues and
    religions—
Jew, Christian, idolater, Frank, Mussulman :
Ah, a horrible sight was Kioff that night !
The gates were all taken—no chance e'en of flight ;
And with torch and with axe the bloody Cossacks
Went hither and thither a-hunting in packs :
They slashed and they slew both Christian and
    Jew—
Women and children, they slaughtered them too.
Some, saving their throats, plunged into the moats,
Or the river—but oh, they had burned all the
    boats !

      *   *   *   *   *

But here let us pause—for I can't pursue further
This scene of rack, ravishment, ruin, and murther.
Too well did the cunning old Cossack succeed !
His plan of attack was successful indeed !
The night was his own—the town it was gone ;
'Twas a heap still a-burning of timber and stone.
One building alone had escaped from the fires,
Saint Sophy's fair church, with its steeples and
    spires.
       Calm, stately, and white,
       It stood in the light ;
And as if 'twould defy all the conqueror's power,—
       As if naught had occurred,
       Might clearly be heard
The chimes ringing soberly every half-hour !

XVI.

[How the Cossack chief bade them burn the church too.—
How they stormed it : and of Hyacinth, his anger
thereat.]

The city was defunct—silence succeeded
    Unto its last fierce agonizing yells ;
And then it was the conqueror first heeded
    The sound of these calm bells.
Furious toward his aides-de-camp he turns,
    And (speaking as if Byron's works he knew)
"Villains !" he fiercely cries, "the city burns,
    Why not the temple too ?
Burn me yon church, and murder all within !"
    The Cossacks thundered at the outer door ;
And Father Hyacinth, who heard the din,
(And thought himself and brethren in distress,
Deserted by their lady patroness)
    Did to her statue turn, and thus his woes out-
      pour.

XVII.

[His prayer to the Saint Sophia.—The statue suddenlie
speaks ; but is interrupted by the breaking in of the
Cossacks.—Of Hyacinth, his courageous address :
and preparation for dying.—Saint Sophia, her speech.
—She gets on the prior's shoulder straddleback, and
bids him run.]

"And is it thus, O falsest of the saints,
    Thou hearest our complaints ?
Tell me, did ever my attachment falter
    To serve thy altar ?
Was not thy name, ere ever I did sleep,
    The last upon my lip ?
Was not thy name the very first that broke
    From me when I awoke ?
Have I not tried with fasting, flogging, penance,
    And mortified counténance

For to find favor, Sophy, in thy sight?
  And lo ! this night,
Forgetful of my prayers and thine own promise,
  Thou turnest from us ;
Lettest the heathen enter in our city,
  And without pity,
Murder our burghers, seize upon their spouses,
  Burn down their houses !
Is such a breach of faith to be endured ?
  See what a lurid
Light from the insolent invader's torches
  Shines on your porches !
E'en now, with thundering battering-ram and
    hammer
  And hideous clamor,
With axemen, swordsmen, pikemen, billmen,
    bowmen,
  The conquering foemen,
O Sophy ! beat your gate about your ears,
  Alas ! and here's
A humble company of pious men,
  Like muttons in a pen,
Whose souls shall quickly from their bodies be
    thrusted.
  Because in you they trusted.
Do you not know the Calmuc chief's desires—
  KILL ALL THE FRIARS !
And you, of all the saints most false and fickle,
  Leave us in this abominable pickle."
" RASH HYACINTHUS !"
  (Here to the astonishment of all her backers,
Saint Sophy, opening wide her wooden jaws,
  Like to a pair of German walnut-crackers,
Began), " I did not think you had been thus,—
O monk of little faith ! Is it because
A rascal scum of filthy Cossack heathen
Besiege our town, that you distrust in *me*, then ?

Think'st thou that I, who in a former day
Did walk across the sea of Marmora
(Not mentioning, for shortness, other seas),—
That I, who skimmed the broad Borysthenes,
Without so much as wetting of my toes,
Am frightened at a set of men like *those?*
I have a mind to leave you to your fate :
Such cowardice as this my scorn inspires."

    Saint Sophy was here
      Cut short in her words,—
For at this very moment in tumbled the gate,
    And with a wild cheer,
      And a clashing of swords,
Swift through the church porches,
With a waving of torches,
And a shriek and a yell
Like the devils of hell,
With pike and with axe
In rushed the Cossacks,—
In rushed the Cossacks, crying, " MURDER THE
    FRIARS !"

Ah ! what a thrill felt Hyacinth,
    When he heard that villainous shout Calmuc !
Now, thought he, my trial beginneth ;
    Saints, O give me courage and pluck !
" Courage, boys, 'tis useless to funk !"
    Thus unto the friars he began :
" Never let it be said that a monk
    Is not likewise a gentleman.
Though the patron saint of the church,
    Spite of all that we've done and we've pray'd,
Leaves us wickedly here in the lurch,
    Hang it, gentlemen, who's afraid ?"

As thus the gallant Hyacinthus spoke,
    He, with an air as easy and as free as

If the quick-coming murder were a joke,
Folded his robes around his sides, and took
Place under sainted Sophy's legs of oak,
    Like Cæsar at the statue of Pompeius.
The monks no leisure had about to look
(Each being absorbed in his particular case),
Else had they seen with what celestial grace
A wooden smile stole o'er the saint's mahogany
       face.

" Well done, well done, Hyacinthus, my son !"
    Thus spoke the sainted statue.
" Though you doubted me in the hour of need,
And spoke of me very rude indeed,
You deserve good luck for showing such pluck,
    And I won't be angry at you."

The monks by-standing, one and all,
    Of this wondrous scene beholders,
    To this kind promise listened content,
    And couldn't contain their astonishment,
    When Saint Sophia moved and went
Down from her wooden pedestal,
    And twisted her legs, sure as eggs is eggs,
    Round Hyacinthus' shoulders !

" Ho ! forward," cries Sophy, "there's no time
    for waiting,
The Cossacks are breaking the very last gate in .
See, the glare of their torches shines red through
    the grating ;
    We've still the back door, and two minutes
    or more.
Now, boys, now or never, we must make for the
    river,
    For we only are safe on the opposite shore.
Run swiftly to-day, lads, if ever you ran,—
Put out your best leg, Hyacinthus, my man ;

And I'll lay five to two that you carry us through,
  Only scamper as fast as you can."

XVIII.

[He runneth, and the Tartars after him.—How the friars sweated, and the pursuers fixed arrows into their tayls.—How, at the last gasp, the friars won, and jumped into Borysthenes fluvius.]

Away went the priest through the little back
  door,
And light on his shoulders the image he bore :
  The honest old priest was not punished the
    least,
Though the image was eight feet, and he meas-
  ured four.
Away went the prior, and the monks at his tail
Went snorting, and puffing, and panting full sail;
  And just as the last at the back door had
    passed,
In furious hunt behold at the front
The Tartars so fierce, with their terrible cheers ;
With axes, and halberts, and muskets, and
  spears,
With torches a-flaming the chapel now came in.
They tore up the mass-book, they stamped on the
  psalter,
They pulled the gold crucifix down from the
  altar ;
The vestments they burned with their blasphem-
  ous fires,
And many cried, "Curse on them ! where are
  the friars ?"
When loaded with plunder, yet seeking for more,
One chanced to fling open the little back door,
Spied out the friars' white robes and long shad-
    ows
In the moon, scampering over the meadows.

And stopped the Cossacks in the midst of their
    arsons,
By crying out lustily, "THERE GO THE PAR-
    SONS !"
With a whoop and a yell, and a scream and a
    shout,
At once the whole murderous body turned out ;
And swift as the hawk pounces down on the
    pigeon,
Pursued the poor short-winded men of religion.

When the sound of that cheering came to the
    monks' hearing,
    O Heaven ! how the poor fellows panted and
      blew !
At fighting not cunning, unaccustomed to run-
    ning,
    When the Tartars came up, what the deuce
      should they do ?
"They'll make us all martyrs, those blood-thirsty
    Tartars !"
    Quoth fat Father Peter to fat Father Hugh.
The shouts they came clearer, the foe they drew
    nearer ;
    Oh, how the bolts whistled, and how the lights
      shone !
"I cannot get further, this running is murther ;
    Come carry me, some one !" cried big Father
      John.
And even the statue grew frightened : "Od rat
    you !"
    It cried, "Mr. Prior, I wish you'd get on !"
On tugged the good friar, but nigher and nigher
Appeared the fierce Russians, with sword and
    with fire.
On tugged the good prior at Saint Sophy's de-
    sire,—

A scramble through bramble, through mud, and
    through mire,
The swift arrows' whizziness causing a dizziness.
Nigh done his business, fit to expire,
Father Hyacinth tugged, and the monks they
    tugged after :
The foemen pursued with a horrible laughter,
And hurl'd their long spears round the poor
    brethren's ears
So true, that next day in the coat of each priest,
Though never a wound was given, there were
    found
        A dozen arrows at least.

    Now the chase seemed at its worst,
    Prior and monks were fit to burst ;
    Scarce you knew the which was first,
       Or pursuers or pursued ;
    When the statue, by Heaven's grace,
    Suddenly did change the face
    Of this interesting race,
       As a saint, sure, only could.

For as the jockey who at Epsom rides,
    When that his steed is spent and punished
    sore,
Diggeth his heels into the courser's sides,
    And thereby makes him run one or two fur-
    longs more ;
    Even thus, betwixt the eighth rib and the
    ninth,
The saint rebuked the prior, that weary creeper ;
    Fresh strength into his limbs her kicks im-
    parted,
    One bound he made, as gay as when he started.
Yes, with his brethren clinging at his cloak,
The statue on his shoulders—fit to choke—

One most tremendous bound made Hyacinth,
And soused friars, statue, and all, slapdash in·
to the Dnieper!

XIX.

[And how the Russians saw the statue get off Hyacinth
his back, and sit down with the friars on Hyacinth
his cloak.—How in this manner of boat they sayled
away.]

And when the Russians, in a fiery rank,
    Panting and fierce, drew up along the shore ;
    (For here the vain pursuing they forbore,
Nor cared they to surpass the river's bank,)
Then, looking from the rocks and rushes dank,
    A sight they witnessed never seen before,
And which, with its accompaniments glorious,
Is writ i' the golden book, or *liber aureus.*

Plump in the Dneiper flounced the friar and
        friends,—
    They dangling round his neck, he fit to choke,
    When suddenly his most miraculous cloak
Over the billowy waves itself extends,
Down from his shoulders quietly descends
    The venerable Sophy's statue of oak ;
Which, sitting down upon the cloak so ample,
Bids all the brethren follow its example !

Each at her bidding sat, and sat at ease ;
    The statue 'gan a gracious conversation,
    And (waving to the foe a salutation)
Sail'd with her wondering happy protégés
Gaily adown the wide Borysthenes,
    Until they came unto some friendly nation.
And when the heathen had at length grown shy
    of

Their conquest, she one day came back again to
  Kioff.

XX.

[Finis, or the end.]

THINK NOT, O READER, THAT WE'RE LAUGH-
  ING AT YOU ;
YOU MAY GO TO KIOFF NOW AND SEE THE
  STATUE !

TITMARSH'S CARMEN LILLIENSE.

LILLE, *Sept.* 2, 1843.

My heart is weary, my peace is gone,
  How shall I e'er my woes reveal?
I have no money, I lie in pawn,
  A stranger in the town of Lille.

I.

WITH twenty pounds but three weeks since
  From Paris forth did Titmarsh wheel,
I thought myself as rich a prince
  As beggar poor I'm now at Lille.

Confiding in my ample means—
  In troth, I was a happy chiel !
I passed the gates of Valenciennes,
  I never thought to come by Lille.

I never thought my twenty pounds
  Some rascal knave would dare to steal ;
I gayly passed the Belgic bounds
  At Quiévrain. twenty miles from Lille.

To Antwerp town I hastened post,
    And as I took my evening meal
I felt my pouch,—my purse was lost,
    O Heaven! Why came I not by Lille?

I straightway called for ink and pen,
    To grandmamma I made appeal;
Meanwhile a loan of guineas ten
    I borrowed from a friend so leal.

I got the cash from grandmamma
    (Her gentle heart my woes could feel),
But where I went and what I saw,
    What matters? Here I am at Lille.

My heart is weary, my peace is gone,
    How shall I e'er my woes reveal?
I have no cash, I lie in pawn,
    A stranger in the town of Lille.

II.

To stealing I can never come,
    To pawn my watch I'm too genteel:
Besides, I left my watch at home—
    How could I pawn it then at Lille?

" *La note,*" at times the guests will say.
    I turn as white as cold boil'd veal;
I turn and look another way,
    I dare not ask the bill at Lille.

I dare not to the landlord say,
    "Good sir, I cannot pay your bill;"
He thinks I am a Lord Anglais,
    And is quite proud I stay at Lille.

He thinks I am a Lord Anglais,
  Like Rothschild or Sir Robert Peel,
And so he serves me every day
  The best of meat and drink in Lille.

Yet when he looks me in the face
  I blush as red as cochineal ;
And think, did he but know my case,
  How changed he'd be, my host of Lille.

My heart is weary, my peace is gone,
  How shall I e'er my woes reveal ?
I have no money, I lie in pawn,
  A stranger in the town of Lille.

III.

The sun bursts out in furious blaze,
  I perspire from head to heel ;
I'd like to hire a one-horse chaise—
  How can I, without cash at Lille ?

I pass in sunshine burning hot
  By cafés where in beer they deal ;
I think how pleasant were a pot,
  A frothing pot of beer of Lille !

What is yon house with walls so thick,
  All girt around with guard and grille ?
O gracious gods ! it makes me sick,
  It is the *prison-house* of Lille !

O cursed prison strong and barred,
  It does my very blood congeal !
I tremble as I pass the guard,
  And quit that ugly part of Lille.

The church-door beggar whines and prays
 I turn away at his appeal :
Ah, church-door beggar ! go thy ways !
 You're not the poorest man in Lille.

My heart is weary, my peace is gone,
 How shall I e'er my woes reveal ?
I have no money, I lie in pawn,
 A stranger in the town of Lille.

IV.

Say, shall I to yon Flemish church,
 And at a Popish altar kneel ?
O, do not leave me in the lurch,—
 I'll cry, ye patron-saints of Lille !

Ye virgins dressed in satin hoops,
 Ye martyrs slain for mortal weal,
Look kindly down ! before you stoops
 The miserablest man in Lille.

And lo ! as I beheld with awe
 A pictured saint (I swear 'tis real),
It smiled, and turned to grandmamma !—
 It did ! and I had hope in Lille !

'Twas five o'clock, and I could eat,
 Although I could not pay my meal :
I hasten back into the street
 Where lies my inn, the best in Lille.

What see I on my table stand,—
 A letter with a well-known seal ?
'Tis grandmamma's ! I know her hand,—
 "To Mr. M. A. Titmarsh, Lille."

I feel a choking in my throat,
  I pant and stagger, faint and reel !
It is -it is—a ten-pound note,
  And I'm no more in pawn at Lille !

[He goes off by the diligence that evening, and is restored
to the bosom of his happy family.]

———

JEAMES OF BUCKLEY SQUARE.

A HELIGY.

COME all ye gents vot cleans the plate,
  Come all ye ladies, maids so fair—
Vile I a story vill relate
  Of cruel Jeames of Buckley Square.
A tighter lad, it is confest,
  Neer valked with powder in his air,
Or vore a nosegay in his breast,
  Than andsum Jeames of Buckley Square.

O Evns ! it was the best of sights,
  Behind his Master's coach and pair,
To see our Jeames in red plush tights,
  A driving hoff from Buckley Square.
He vel became his hagwilletts,
  He cocked his at with *such* a hair ;
His calves and viskers *vas* such pets,
  That hall loved Jeames of Buckley Square.

He pleased the hup-stairs folks as vell,
  And o ! I vithered vith despair,
Missis *vould* ring the parler bell,
  And call up Jeames in Buckley Square.

Both beer and sperrits he abhord,
   (Sperrits and beer I can't a bear,)
You would have thought he vas a lord
   Down in our All in Buckley Square.

Last year he visper'd, " Mary Ann,
   Ven I've an under'd pound to spare,
To take a public is my plan,
   And leave this hojous Buckley Square."
O how my gentle heart did bound,
   To think that I his name should bear !
" Dear Jeames," says I, " I've twenty pound,"
   And gev them him in Buckley Square.

Our master vas a City gent,
   His name's in railroads everywhere,
And lord, vot lots of letters vent
   Betwigst his brokers and Buckley Square :
My Jeames it was the letters took,
   And read them all (I think it's fair),
And took a leaf from Master's book,
   As *hothers* do in Buckley Square.

Encouraged with my twenty pound,
   Of which poor *I* was unavare,
He wrote the Companies all round,
   And signed hisself from Buckley Square.
And how John Porter used to grin,
   As day by day, share after share,
Came railvay letters pouring in,
   " J. Plush, Esquire, in Buckley Square.

Our servants' All was in a rage—
   Scrip, stock, curves, gradients, bull and
      bear,
Vith butler, coachman, groom and page,
   Vas all the talk in Buckley Square.

But O ! imagine vot I felt
　　Last Vensday veek as ever were ;
I gits a letter, which I spelt
　　" Miss M. A. Hoggins, Buckley Square."

He sent me back my money true—
　　He sent me back my lock of air,
And said, " My dear, I bid ajew
　　To Mary Hann and Buckley Square.
Think not to marry, foolish Hann,
　　With people who your betters are ;
James Plush is now a gentleman,
　　And you—a cook in Buckley Square.

" I've thirty thousand guineas won,
　　In six short months, by genus rare
You little thought what Jeames was on,
　　Poor Mary Hann, in Buckley Square.
I've thirty thousand guineas net,
　　Powder and plush I scorn to vear ;
And so, Miss Mary Hann, forget
　　For hever Jeames of Buckley Square."

————

LINES UPON MY SISTER'S PORTRAIT.

BY THE LORD SOUTHDOWN.

THE castle towers of Bareacres are fair upon the
　　lea,
Where the cliffs of bonny Diddlesex rise up from
　　out the sea :
I stood upon the donjon keep and view'd the
　　country o'er,
I saw the lands of Bareacres for fifty miles or
　　more.

I stood upon the donjon keep—it is a sacred
  place—
Where floated for eight hundred years the banner
  of my race ;
Argent, a dexter sinople, and gules an azure
  field :
There ne'er was nobler cognizance on knightly
  warrior's shield.

The first time England saw the shield 'twas round
  a Norman neck,
On board a ship from Valery, King William was
  on deck.
A Norman lance the colors wore, in Hastings'
  fatal fray—
St. Willibald for Bareacres ! 'twas double gules
  that day !
O Heaven and sweet St. Willibald ! in many a
  battle since
A loyal-hearted Bareacres has ridden by his Prince!
At Acre with Plantagenet, with Edward at
  Poictiers,
The pennon of the Bareacres was foremost on
  the spears !

'Twas pleasant in the battle-shock to hear our
  war-cry ringing :
O grant me, sweet St.Willibald, to listen to such
  singing !
Three hundred steel-clad gentlemen, we drove the
  foe before us,
And thirty score of British bows kept twanging to
  the chorus !
O knights, my noble ancestors ! and shall I never
  hear
St. Willibald for Bareacres through battle ringing
  clear ?

I'd cut me off this strong right hand a single hour
    to ride,
And strike a blow for Barcacres, my fathers, at
    your side !

Dash down, dash down, you mandolin, beloved
    sister mine !
Those blushing lips may never sing the glories
    of our line :
Our ancient castles echo to the clumsy feet of
    churls,
The spinning-jenny houses in the mansion of our
    Earls.
Sing not, sing not, my Angeline ! in days so
    base and vile,
'Twere sinful to be happy, 'twere sacrilege to
    smile.
I'll hie me to my lonely hall, and by its cheerless
    hob
I'll muse on other days, and wish—and wish I
    were—A Snob.

———

LITTLE BILLEE.*

Air—" Il y avait un petit navire."

There were three sailors of Bristol city
    Who took a boat and went to sea.
But first with beef and captain's biscuits
    And pickled pork they loaded she.

* As different versions of this popular song have been set
to music and sung, no apology is needed for the insertion in
these pages of what is considered to be the correct version.

There was gorging Jack and guzzling Jimmy,
  And the youngest he was little Billee.
Now when they got as far as the Equator
  They'd nothing left but one split pea.

Says gorging Jack to guzzling Jimmy,
  " I am extremely hungaree."
To gorging Jack says guzzling Jimmy,
  "We've nothing left, us must eat we."

Says gorging Jack to guzzling Jimmy.
  " With one another we shouldn't agree !
There's little Bill, he's young and tender,
  We're old and tough, so let's eat he.

"Oh ! Billy, we're going to kill and eat you,
  So undo the button of your chemie."
When Bill received this information
  He used his pocket handkerchie.

" First let me say my catechism,
  Which my poor mammy taught to me."
" Make haste, make haste," says guzzling Jimmy,
  While Jack pulled out his snickersnee.

So Billy went up to the main-top-gallant mast,
  And down he fell on his bended knee.
He scarce had come to the twelfth commandment
  When up he jumps.   " There's land I see :

" Jerusalem and Madagascar,
  And North and South Amerikee :
There's the British flag a riding at anchor,
  With Admiral Napier, K.C.B."

So when they got aboard of the Admiral's
  He hanged fat Jack and flogged Jimmee ,

But as for little Bill he made him
The Captain of a Seventy-three.

THE END OF THE PLAY.

THE play is done ; the curtain drops,
  Slow falling to the prompter's bell :
A moment yet the actor stops,
  And looks around, to say farewell.
It is an irksome word and task ;
  And, when he's laughed and said his say,
He shows, as he removes the mask,
  A face that's anything but gay.

One word, ere yet the evening ends,
  Let's close it with a parting rhyme,
And pledge a hand to all young friends,
  As fits the merry Christmas time.*
On life's wide scene you, too, have parts,
  That Fate ere long shall bid you play ;
Good night ! with honest gentle hearts
  A kindly greeting go alway !

Good night !—I'd say, the griefs, the joys,
  Just hinted in this mimic page,
The triumphs and defeats of boys,
  Are but repeated in our age.
I'd say, your woes were not less keen,
  Your hopes more vain, than those of men ;
Your pangs or pleasures of fifteen
  At forty-five played o'er again.

---

* These verses were printed at the end of a Christmas
book (1848-9), " Dr. Birch and his Young Friends."

I'd say, we suffer and we strive,
  Not less nor more as men than boys ;
With grizzled beards at forty-five,
  As erst at twelve in corduroys.
And if, in time of sacred youth,
  We learned at home to love and pray,
Pray Heaven that early Love and Truth
  May never wholly pass away.

And in the world, as in the school,
  I'd say, how fate may change and shift ;
The prize be sometimes with the fool,
  The race not always to the swift.
The strong may yield, the good may fall,
  The great man be a vulgar clown,
The knave be lifted over all,
  The kind cast pitilessly down.

Who knows the inscrutable design ?
  Blessed be He who took and gave !
Why should your mother, Charles, not mine,
  Be weeping at her darling's grave ? *
We bow to Heaven that will'd it so,
  That darkly rules the fate of all,
That sends the respite or the blow,
  That's free to give, or to recall.

This crowns his feast with wine and wit :
  Who brought him to that mirth and state ?
His betters, see, below him sit,
  Or hunger hopeless at the gate.
Who bade the mud from Dives' wheel
  To spurn the rags of Lazarus ?
Come, brother, in that dust we'll kneel,
  Confessing Heaven that ruled it thus.

* C. B. ob. 29th November, 1848, æt. 42.

So each shall mourn, in life's advance,
  Dear hopes, dear friends, untimely killed ;
Shall grieve for many a forfeit chance,
  And longing passion unfulfilled.
Amen ! whatever fate be sent,
  Pray God the heart may kindly glow,
Although the head with cares be bent,
  And whitened with the winter snow.

Come wealth or want, come good or ill,
  Let young and old accept their part,
And bow before the Awful Will,
  And bear it with an honest heart,
Who misses or who wins the prize.
  Go, lose or conquer as you can ;
But if you fail, or if you rise,
  Be each, pray God, a gentleman.

A gentleman, or old or young !
  (Bear kindly with my humble lays);
The sacred chorus first was sung
  Upon the first of Christmas days :
The shepherds heard it overhead—
  The joyful angels raised it then :
Glory to Heaven on high, it said,
  And peace on earth to gentle men.

My song, save this, is little worth ;
  I lay the weary pen aside,
And wish you health, and love, and mirth,
  As fits the solemn Christmas-tide.
As fits the holy Christmas birth,
  Be this, good friends, our carol still—
Be peace on earth, be peace on earth,
  To men of gentle will.

VANITAS VANITATUM.

How spake of old the Royal Seer?
  (His text is one I love to treat on.)
This life of ours, he said, is sheer
  Mataiotes Mataioteton.

O Student of this gilded Book,
  Declare, while musing on its pages,
If truer words were ever spoke
  By ancient or by modern sages?

The various authors' names but note,*
  French, Spanish, English, Russians, Germans ;
And in the volume polyglot
  Sure you may read a hundred sermons !

What histories of life are here,
  More wild than all romancers' stories ;
What wondrous transformations queer,
  What homilies on human glories !

What theme for sorrow or for scorn !
  What chronicle of Fate's surprises—
Of adverse fortune nobly borne,
  Of chances, changes, ruins, rises !

Of thrones upset, and sceptres broke,
  How strange a record here is written !
Of honors, dealt as if in joke ;
  Of brave desert unkindly smitten.

---

* Between a page by Jules Janin, and a poem by the
Turkish Ambassador, in Madame de R——'s album,
containing the autographs of kings, princes, poets, mar-
shals, musicians, diplomatists, statesmen, artists, and men
of letters of all nations.

How low men were, and how they rise!
　How high they were, and how they tumble!
O vanity of vanities!
　O laughable, pathetic jumble!

Here between honest Janin's joke
　And his Turk Excellency's firman,
I write my name upon the book:
　I write my name—and end my sermon.

———

O vanity of vanities!
　How wayward the decrees of Fate are;
How very weak the very wise,
　How very small the very great are!

What mean these stale moralities,
　Sir Preacher, from your desk you mumble?
Why rail against the great and wise,
　And tire us with your ceaseless grumble?

Pray choose us out another text,
　O man morose and narrow-minded!
Come turn the page—I read the next,
　And then the next, and still I find it.

Read here how Wealth aside was thrust,
　And Folly set in place exalted;
How Princes footed in the dust,
　While lackeys in the saddle vaulted.

Though thrice a thousand years are past
　Since David's son, the sad and splendid,
The weary King Ecclesiast,
　Upon his awful tablets penned it,—

Methinks the text is never stale,
    And life is every day renewing
Fresh comments on the old old tale
    Of Folly, Fortune, Glory, Ruin.

Hark to the Preacher, preaching still
    He lifts his voice and cries his sermon,
Here at St. Peter's of Cornhill,
    As yonder on the Mount of Hermon:

For you and me to heart to take
    (O dear beloved brother readers)
To-day as when the good King spake
    Beneath the solemn Syrian cedars.

LOVE-SONGS MADE EASY.

WHAT MAKES MY HEART TO THRILL AND GLOW?

THE MAYFAIR LOVE-SONG.

WINTER and summer, night and morn,
  I languish at this table dark ;
My office window has a corn-
  er looks into St. James's Park.
I hear the foot-guards' bugle-horn,
  Their tramp upon parade I mark ;
I am a gentleman forlorn,
  I am a Foreign-Office Clerk.

My toils, my pleasures, every one,
  I find are stale, and dull, and slow ;
And yesterday, when work was done,
  I felt myself so sad and low,
I could have seized a sentry's gun
  My wearied brains out out to blow.
What is it makes my blood to run ?
  What makes my heart to beat and glow ?

My notes of hand are burnt, perhaps ?
  Some one has paid my tailor's bill ?
No: every morn the tailor raps ;
  My I O U's are extant still.
I still am prey of debt and dun ;
  My elder brother's stout and well.

What is it makes my blood to run ?
　　What makes my heart to glow and swell ?

I know my chief's distrust and hate ;
　　He says I'm lazy and I shirk.
Ah ! had I genius like the late
　　Right Honorable Edmund Burke !
My chance of all promotion's gone,
　　I know it is,—he hates me so.
What is it makes my blood to run,
　　And all my heart to swell and glow ?

Why, why is all so bright and gay ?
　　There is no change, there is no cause ;
My office-time I found to-day
　　Disgusting as it ever was.
At three, I went and tried the Clubs,
　　And yawned and saunter'd to and fro ;
And now my heart jumps up and throbs,
　　And all my soul is in a glow.

At half-past four I had the cab ;
　　I drove as hard as I could go.
The London sky was dirty drab,
　　And dirty brown the London snow.
And as I rattled in a cant-
　　er down by dear old Bolton Row,
A something made my heart to pant,
　　And caused my cheek to flush and glow.

What could it be that made me find
　　Old Jawkins pleasant at the Club ?
Why was it that I laughed and grinned
　　At whist, although I lost the rub ?
What was it made me drink like mad
　　Thirteen small glasses of Curaçao ?
That made my inmost heart so glad,
　　And every fibre thrill and glow ?

She's home again ! she's home, she's home !
  Away all cares and griefs and pain ;
I knew she would—she's back from Rome ;
  She's home again ! she's home again !
"The family's gone abroad," they said,
  September last—they told me so ;
Since then my lonely heart is dead,
  My blood, I think's forgot to flow.

She's home again ! Away all care !
  O fairest form the world can show !
O beaming eyes ! O golden hair !
  O tender voice, that breathes so low !
O gentlest, softest, purest heart !
  O joy, O hope !—"My tiger, ho !"
Fitz-Clarence said ; we saw him start—
  He galloped down to Bolton Row.

———

THE GHAZUL, OR ORIENTAL LOVE-SONG.

THE ROCKS.

I was a timid little antelope ;
My home was in the rocks, the lonely rocks.

I saw the hunters scouring on the plain ;
I lived among the rocks, the lonely rocks.

I was a-thirsty in the summer-heat ;
I ventured to the tents beneath the rocks.

Zuleikah ! brought me water from the well ;
Since then I have been faithless to the rocks.

I saw her face reflected in the well ;
Her camels since have marched into the rocks.

I look to see her image in the well ;
I only see my eyes, my own sad eyes.
My mother is alone among the rocks.

THE MERRY BARD.

ZULEIKAH ! The young Agas in the bazaar are
slim-waisted and wear yellow slippers.   I am old
and hideous.   One of my eyes is out, and the hairs
of my beard are mostly gray.   Praise be to
Allah ! I am a merry bard.

There is a bird upon the terrace of the Emir's
chief wife.   Praise be to Allah ! He has emer-
alds on his neck, and a ruby tail.   I am a merry
bard.   He deafens me with his diabolical screaming.   .

There is a little brown bird in the basket-
maker's cage.   Praise be to Allah ! He ravishes
my soul in the moonlight.   I am a merry bard.

The peacock is an Aga, but the little bird is a
Bulbul.

I am a little brown Bulbul.   Come and listen
in the moonlight.   Praise be to Allah !   I am a
merry bard.

THE CAÏQUE.

YONDER to the kiosk, beside the creek,
Paddle the swift caïque.
Thou brawny oarsman with the sun-burnt cheek,
Quick ! for it soothes my heart to hear the Bulbul
    speak.

Ferry me quickly to the Asian shores,
Swift bending to your oars.
Beneath the melancholy sycamores,
Hark ! what a ravishing note the love-lorn Bulbul
    pours !

Behold, the boughs seem quivering with delight,
The stars themselves more bright,
As mid the waving branches out of sight
The Lover of the Rose sits singing through the
    night.

Under the boughs I sat and listened still,
I could not have my fill.
" How comes," I said, " such music to his bill ?
Tell me for whom he sings so beautiful a trill."

"Once I was dumb," then did the Bird disclose,
" But looked upon the Rose ;
And in the garden where the loved one grows,
I straightway did begin sweet music to compose."

"O bird of song, there's one in this caïque
The Rose would also seek,
So he might learn like you to love and speak."
Then answered me the bird of dusky beak,
" The Rose, the Rose of Love blushes on
    Leilah's cheek."

MY NORA.

BENEATH the gold acacia buds
My gentle Nora sits and broods,
Far, far away in Boston woods
        My gentle Nora !

I see the tear-drop in her e'e,
Her bosom's heaving tenderly ;
I know—I know she thinks of me,
   My darling Nora !

And where am I ? My love, whilst thou
Sitt'st sad beneath the acacia bough,
Where pearl's on neck, and wreath on brow,
   I stand, my Nora !

Mid carcanet and coronet,
Where joy-lamps shine and flowers are set—
Where England's chivalry are met,
   Behold me Nora !

In this strange scene of revelry,
Amidst this gorgeous chivalry,
A form I saw was like to thee,
   My love—my Nora !

She paused amidst her converse glad ;
The lady saw that I was sad,
She pitied the poor lonely lad,—
   Dost love her, Nora?

In sooth, she is a lovely dame,
A lip of red, and eye of flame,
And clustering golden locks, the same
   As thine, dear Nora !

Her glance is softer than the dawn's,
Her foot is lighter than the fawn's,
Her breast is whiter than the swan's,
   Or thine, my Nora !

Oh, gentle breast to pity me !
Oh, lovely Ladye Emily !
Till death – till death I'll think of thee—
   Of thee and Nora !

TO MARY.

I SEEM, in the midst of the crowd,
   The lightest of all ;
My laughter rings cheery and loud
   In banquet and ball.
My lip hath its smiles and its sneers,
   For all men to see ;
But my soul, and my truth, and my tears,
   Are for thee, are for thee !

Around me they flatter and fawn—
   The young and the old,
The fairest are ready to pawn
   Their hearts for my gold.
They sue me—I laugh as I spurn
   The slaves at my knee ;
But in faith and in fondness I turn
   Unto thee, unto thee !

SERENADE.

Now the toils of day are over,
   And the sun hath sunk to rest,
Seeking, like a fiery lover,
   The bosom of the blushing west.

The faithful night keeps watch and ward,
   Raising the moon her silver shield,
And summoning the stars to guard
   The slumbers of my fair Mathilde !

The faithful night ! Now all things lie
  Hid by her mantle dark and dim,
In pious hope I hither hie,
  And humbly chant mine evening hymn.

Thou art my prayer, my saint, my shrine !
  (For never holy pilgrim kneel'd
Or wept at feet more pure than thine),
  My virgin love, my sweet Mathilde !

FIVE GERMAN DITTIES.

A TRAGIC STORY.

BY ADELBERT VON CHAMISSO.

" ——'s war Einer, dem's zu Herzen gieng."

THERE lived a sage in days of yore,
And he a handsome pigtail wore ;
But wondered much and sorrowed more
  Because it hung behind him.

He mused upon this curious case,
And swore he'd change the pigtail's place,
And have it hanging at his face,
  Not dangling there behind him.

Says he, " The mystery I've found,—
I'll turn me round,"—he turned him round ;
  But still it hung behind him.

Then round, and round, and out and in,
All day the puzzled sage did spin ;
In vain—it mattered not a pin,—
  The pigtail hung behind him.

And right, and left, and round about,
And up, and down, and in, and out.
He turned ; but still the pigtail stout
  Hung steadily behind him.

And though his efforts never slack,
And though he twist, and whirl, and tack,
Alas ! still faithful to his back
    The pigtail hangs behind him.

———

THE CHAPLET.

FROM UHLAND.

" Es pflückte Blümlein mannigfalt."

A LITTLE girl through field and wood
    Went plucking flowerets here and there,
When suddenly beside her stood
    A lady wondrous fair.

The lovely lady smiled, and laid
    A wreath upon the maiden's brow :
" Wear it ; 'twill blossom soon," she said,
    " Although 'tis leafless now."

The little maiden older grew
    And wandered forth of moonlight eves,
And sighed and loved as maids will do ;
    When, lo ! her wreath bore leaves.

Then was our maid a wife, and hung
    Upon a joyful bridegroom's bosom ;
When from the garland's leaves there sprung
    Fair store of blossom.

And presently a baby fair
    Upon her gentle breast she reared ;
When midst the wreath that bound her hair
    Rich golden fruit appeared.

But when her love lay cold in death,
  Sunk in the black and silent tomb,
All sere and withered was the wreath
  That wont so bright to bloom.

Yet still the withered wreath she wore ;
  She wore it at her dying hour ;
When, lo ! the wondrous garland bore
  Both leaf, and fruit, and flower !

————

THE KING ON THE TOWER.

FROM UHLAND.

"**Da liegen sie alle, die grauen Höhen.**"

THE cold gray hills they bind me around,
  The darksome valleys lie sleeping below,
But the winds, as they pass o'er all this ground,
  Bring me never a sound of woe.

Oh ! for all I have suffered and striven,
  Care has embittered my cup and my feast ;
But here is the night and the dark blue heaven,
  And my soul shall be at rest.

O golden legends writ in the skies !
  I turn toward you with longing soul,
And list to the awful harmonies
  Of the Spheres as on they roll.

My hair is gray and my sight nigh gone ;
  My sword it rusteth upon the wall ;
Right have I spoken, and right have I done :
  When shall I rest me once for all ?

O blessed rest ! O royal night !
Wherefore seemeth the time so long
Till I see yon stars in their fullest light,
And list to their loudest song?

TO A VERY OLD WOMAN.

LA MOTTE FOUQUÉ.

" Und Du gingst einst, die Myrt' im Haare."

AND thou wert once a maiden fair,
    A blushing virgin warm and young:
With myrtles wreathed in golden hair,
And glossy brow that knew no care—
    Upon a bridegroom's arm you hung.

The golden locks are silvered now,
    The blushing cheek is pale and wan ;
The spring may bloom, the autumn glow,
All's one—in chimney corner thou
    Sitt'st shivering on.—

A moment—and thou sink'st to rest !
To wake perhaps an angel blest
    In the bright presence of thy Lord
Oh, weary is life's path to all !
Hard is the strife, and light the fall,
    But wondrous the reward !

A CREDO.

I.

For the sole edification
Of this decent congregation,
Goodly people, by your grant
I will sing a holy chant—
    I will sing a holy chant.
If the ditty sound but oddly,
'Twas a father, wise and godly,
    Sang it so long ago—
Then sing as Martin Luther sang:
" Who loves not wine, woman, and song,
He is a fool his whole life long !"

II.

He, by custom patriarchal,
Loved to see the beaker sparkle ;
And he thought the wine improved,
Tasted by the lips he loved—
    By the kindly lips he loved.
Friends, I wish this custom pious
Duly were observed by us,
    To combine love, song, wine,
And sing as Martin Luther sang,
As Doctor Martin Luther sang:
"Who loves not wine, woman, and song,
He is a fool his whole life-long !"

III.

Who refuses this our Credo,
And who will not sing as we do,
Were he holy as John Knox,
I'd pronounce him heterodox !
    I'd pronounce him heterodox,

And from out this congregation,
With a solemn commination,
   Banish quick the heretic,
Who will not sing as Luther sang,
As Doctor Martin Luther sang :
'' Who loves not wine, woman, and song,
He is a fool his whole life long !''

FOUR
IMITATIONS OF BERANGER.

LE ROI D'YVETOT.

IL était un roi d'Yvetot,
   Peu connu dans l'histoire ;
Se levant tard, se couchant tôt,
   Dormant fort bien sans gloire,
Et couronné par Jeanneton
D'un simple bonnet de coton,
      Dit-on.
    Oh ! oh ! oh ! oh ! ah ! ah ! ah ! ah!
    Quel bon petit roi c'était là !
     La, la.

Il fesait ses quatre repas
   Dans son palais de chaume,
Et sur un âne, pas à pas,
   Parcourait son royaume.
Joyeux, simple et croyant le bien,
Pour toute garde il n'avait rien
     Qu'un chien.
    Oh ! oh ! oh ! oh ! ah ! ah ! ah ! ah ! &c.

Il n'avait de goût onéreux
   Qu'une soif un deu vive ;
Mais, en rendant son peuple heureux,
   Il faut bien qu'un roi vive,

Lui-même à table, et sans suppôt,
Sur chaque muid levait un pot
      D'impôt.
   Oh ! oh ! oh ! oh ! ah ! ah ! ah ! ah ! &c.

Aux filles de bonnes maisons
   Comme il avait su plaire,
Ses sujets avaient cent raisons
   De le nommer leur père :
D'ailleurs il ne levait de ban
Que pour tirer quatre fois l'an
      Au blanc,
   Oh ! oh ! oh ! oh ! ah ! ah ! ah ! ah ! &c.

Il n'agrandit point ses états,
   Fut un voisin commode,
Et, modèle des potentats,
   Prit le plaisir pour code,
Ce n'est que lorsqu'il expira,
Que le peuple qui l'enterra
      Pleura.
   Oh ! oh ! oh ! oh ! ah ! ah ! ah ! ah ! &c.

On conserve encor le portrait
   De ce digne et bon prince ;
C'est l'enseigne d'un carbaret
   Fameux dans la province.
Les jours de fête, bien souvent,
La foule s'écrie en buvant
      Devant :
   Oh ! oh ! oh ! oh ! ah ! ah ! ah ! ah ! &c.

———

THE KING YVETOT.

THERE was a king of Yvetot,
   Of whom renown hath little said,

Who let all thoughts of glory go,
  And dawdled half his days a-bed ;
And every night, as night came round,
By Jenny with a nightcap crowned,
          Slept very sound :
        Sing ho, ho, ho ! and he, he, he !
        That's the kind of king for me.

And every day it came to pass,
  That four lusty meals made he ;
And step by step, upon an ass,
  Rode abroad, his realms to see ;
And wherever he did stir,
What think you was his escort, sir ?
          Why, an old cur.
        Sing ho, ho, ho ! &c.

If e'er he went into excess,
  'Twas from a somewhat lively thirst ;
But he who would his subjects bless,
  Odd's fish !—must wet his whistle first ;
And so from every cask they got,
Our king did to himself allot
          At least a pot.
        Sing ho, ho ! &c.

To all the ladies of the land,
  A courteous king, and kind, was he—
The reason why, you'll understand,
  They named him Pater Patriæ.
Each year he called his fighting men,
And marched a league from home, and then
          Marched back again,
        Sing ho, ho ! &c.

Neither by force nor false pretence,
  He sought to make his kingdom great,

And made (O princes, learn from hence)—
" Live and let live," his rule of state.
'Twas only when he came to die,
That his people who stood by,
                    Were known to cry.
        Sing ho, ho ! &c.

The portrait of this best of kings
    Is extant still, upon a sign
That on a village tavern swings,
    Famed in the country for good wine.
The people in their Sunday trim,
Filling their glasses to the brim,
                    Look up to him,
        Singing ha, ha, ha ! and he, he, he !
        That's the sort of king for me.

THE KING OF BRENTFORD.

ANOTHER VERSION.

THERE was a king in Brentford,—of whom no
    legends tell,
But who, without his glory, —could eat and sleep
    right well.
His Polly's cotton nightcap,—it was his crown
    of state,
He slept of evenings early,—and rose of mornings
    late.

All in a fine mud palace,—each day he took four
    meals,
And for a guard of honor—a dog ran at his heels,
Sometimes to view his kingdoms,—rode forth this
    monarch good,
And then a prancing jackass—he royally bestrod.

There were no costly habits—with which this
    king was curst,
Except (and where's the harm on't?)—a some-
    what lively thirst;
But people must pay taxes,—and kings must
    have their sport,
So out of every gallon—His Grace he took a
    quart.

He pleased the ladies round him,—with manners
    soft and bland;
With reason good, they named him—the father
    of his land.
Each year his mighty armies—marched forth in
    gallant show;
Their enemies were targets,—their bullets they
    were tow.

He vexed no quiet neighbor,—no useless con-
    quest made,
But by the laws of pleasure—his peaceful realm
    he swayed.
And in the years he reigned,—through all this
    country wide,
There was no cause for weeping,—save when
    the good man died.

The faithful men of Brentford—do still their
    king deplore,
His portrait yet is swinging—beside an alehouse
    door.
And topers, tender-hearted,—regard his honest
    phiz,
And envy times departed,—that knew a reign
    like his.

LE GRENIER.

Je viens revoir l'asile où ma jeunesse
De la misère a subi les leçons.
J'avais vingt ans, une folle maîtresse,
De francs amis et l'amour des chansons.
Bravant le monde et les sots et les sages,
Sans avenir, riche de mon printemps,
Leste et joyeux je montais six étages.
Dans un grenier qu'on est bien à vingt ans !

C'est un grenier, point ne veux qu'on l'ignore,
Là fut mon lit, bien chétif et bien dur ;
Là fut ma table ; et je retrouve encore
Trois pieds d'un vers charbonnés sur le mur.
Apparaissez, plaisirs de mon bel âge,
Que d'un coup d'aile a fustigés le temps :
Vingt fois pour vous j'ai mis ma montre en gage,
Dans un grenier qu'on est bien à vingt ans !

Lisette ici doit surtout apparaître,
Vive, jolie, avec un frais chapeau ;
Déjà sa main à l'étroite fenêtre
Suspend son schal, en guise de rideau.
Sa robe aussi va parer ma couchette ;
Respecte, Amour, ses plis longs et flottans.
J'ai su depuis qui payait sa toilette.
Dans un grenier qu'on est bien à vingt ans !

A table un jour, jour de grande richesse,
De mes amis les voix brillaient en chœur,
Quand jusqu'ici monte un cri d'allégresse :
A Marengo Bonaparte est vainqueur.
Le canon gronde ; un autre chant commence ;
Nous célébrons tant de faits éclatans.
Les rois jamais n'envahiront la France,
Dans un grenier qu'on est bien à vingt ans !

Quittons ce toit où ma raison s'énivre.
Oh ! quil's sont loin ces jours si regrettés !
J'échangerais ce qu'il me reste à vivre
Contre un des mois qu'ici Dieu m'a comptés,
Pour rêver gloire, amour, plaisir, folie,
Pour dépenser sa vie en peu d'instans,
D'un long espoir pour la voir embellie.
Dans un grenier qu'on est bien à vingt ans !

———

THE GARRET.

WITH pensive eyes the little room I view,
    Where, in my youth, I weathered it so long,
With a wild mistress, a stanch friend or two,
    And a light heart still breaking into song :
Making a mock of life, and all its cares,
    Rich in the glory of my rising sun,
Lightly I vaulted up four pair of stairs,
    In the brave days when I was twenty-one.

Yes ; 'tis a garret—let him know't who will—
    There was my bed—full hard it was and small ;
My table there—and I decipher still
    Half a lame couplet charcoaled on the wall.
Ye joys, that Time hath swept with him away,
    Come to mine eyes, ye dreams of love and fun ;
For you I pawned my watch how many a day,
    In the brave days when I was twenty-one.

And see my little Jessy, first of all ;
    She comes with pouting lips and sparkling
        eyes :
Behold, how roguishly she pins her shawl
    Across the narrow casement, curtain-wise :

Now by the bed her petticoat glides down,
  And when did women look the worse in none ?
I have heard since who paid for many a gown,
  In the brave days when I was twenty-one.

One jolly evening, when my friends and I
  Made happy music with our songs and cheers,
A shout of triumph mounted up thus high,
  And distant cannon opened on our ears ;
We rise,—we join in the triumphant strain,—
  Napoleon conquers—Austerlitz is won—
Tyrants shall never tread us down again,
  In the brave days when I was twenty-one.

Let us begone—the place is sad and strange—
  How far, far off, these happy times appear ;
All that I have to live I'd gladly change
  For one such month as I have wasted here—
To draw long dreams of beauty, love, and power,
  From founts of hope that never will outrun,
And drink all life's quintessence in an hour,
  Give me the days when I was twenty-one.

———

ROGER-BONTEMPS.

Aux gens atrabilaires
Pour exemple donné,
En un temps de misères
Roger-Bontemps est né.
Vivre obscur à sa guise,
Narguer les mécontens ;
Eh gai ! c'est la devise
Du gros Roger-Bontemps.

Du chapeau de son père
Coiffé dans les grands jours,
De roses ou de lierre
Le rajeunir toujours ;
Mettre un manteau de bure,
Vieil ami de vingt ans ;
Eh gai ! c'est la parure
Du gros Roger-Bontemps.

Posséder dans sa hutte
Une table, un vieux lit,
Des cartes, une flûte,
Un broc que Dieu remplit ;
Un portrait de maîtresse,
Un coffre et rien dedans ;
Eh gai ! c'est la richesse
Du gros Roger-Bontemps.

Aux enfans de la ville
Montrer de petits jeux ;
Etre fesseur habile
De contes graveleux ;
Ne parler que de danse
Et d'almanachs chantans :
Eh gai ! c'est la science
Du gros Roger-Bontemps.

Faute de vins d'élite,
Sabler ceux du canton :
Préférer Marguerite
Aux dames du grand ton :
De joie et de tendresse
Remplir tous ses instans :
Eh gai ! c'est la sagesse
Du gros Roger-Bontemps.

Dire au ciel : Je me fie,
Mon père, à ta bonté ;

De ma philosophie
Pardonne le gaîté :
Que ma saison dernière
Soit encore un printemps ;
Eh gai ! c'est la prière
Du gros Roger-Bontemps.

Vous pauvres pleins d'envie,
Vous riches désireux,
Vous, dont le char dévie
Après un cours heureux ;
Vous, qui perdrez peut-être
Des titres éclatans,
Eh gai ! prenez pour maître
Le gros Roger-Bontemps.

JOLLY JACK.

WHEN fierce political debate
    Throughout the isle was storming,
And Rads attacked the throne and state,
    And Tories the reforming,
To claim the furious rage of each,
    And right the land demented,
Heaven sent us Jolly Jack, to teach
    The way to be contented.

Jack's bed was straw, 'twas warm and soft,
    His chair, a three-legged stool ;
His broken jug was emptied oft,
    Yet, somehow, always full.
His mistress' portrait decked the wall,
    His mirror had a crack ;
Yet, gay and glad, though this was all
    His wealth, lived Jolly Jack.

To give advice to avarice,
  Teach pride its mean condition,
And preach good sense to dull pretence,
  Was honest Jack's high mission.
Our simple statesman found his rule
  Of moral in the flagon,
And held his philosophic school
  Beneath the " George and Dragon."

When village Solons cursed the Lords,
  And called the malt-tax sinful,
Jack heeded not their angry words,
  But smiled and drank his skinful.
And when men wasted health and life
  In search of rank and riches,
Jack marked aloof the paltry strife,
  And wore his threadbare breeches.

" I enter not the church," he said,
  " But I'll not seek to rob it ;"
So worthy Jack Joe Miller read,
  While others studied Cobbett.
His talk it was of feast and fun ;
  His guide the Almanack ;
From youth to age thus gayly run
  The life of Jolly Jack.

And when Jack prayed, as oft he would,
  He humbly thanked his Maker ;
" I am," said he, " O Father good !
  Nor Catholic nor Quaker :
Give each his creed, let each proclaim
  His catalogue of curses ;
I trust in Thee, and not in them,
  In Thee and in Thy mercies !

" Forgive me if, midst all Thy works,
  No hint I see of damning ;

And think there's faith among the Turks,
  And hope for e'en the Brahmin.
Harmless my mind is, and my mirth,
  And kindly is my laughter ;
I cannot see the smiling earth,
  And think there's hell hereafter."

Jack died ; he left no legacy,
  Save that his story teaches :—
Content to peevish poverty ;
  Humility to riches.
Ye scornful great, ye envious small,
  Come follow in his track ;
We all were happier, if we all
  Would copy JOLLY JACK.

IMITATION OF HORACE.

TO HIS SERVING BOY.

PERSICOS odi,
Puer, apparatus ;
Displicent nexæ
Philyrâ coronæ :
Mitte sectari,
Rosa quo locorum
Sera moretur.

Simplici myrto
Nihil allabores
Sedulus, curo :
Neque te ministrum
Dedecet myrtus,
Neque me sub arctâ
Vite bibentem.

AD MINISTRAM.

DEAR Lucy, you know what my wish is,—
I hate all your Frenchified fuss :
Your silly entrées and made dishes
Were never intended for us.

No footman in lace and in ruffles
   Need dangle behind my arm-chair ;
And never mind seeking for truffles,
   Although they be ever so rare.

But a plain leg of mutton, my Lucy,
   I prithee get ready at three :
Have it smoking, and tender and juicy,
   And what better meat can there be ?
And when it has feasted the master,
   'Twill amply suffice for the maid ;
Meanwhile I will smoke my canaster,
   And tipple my ale in the shade.

OLD FRIENDS WITH NEW FACES.

THE KNIGHTLY GUERDON.*

UNTRUE to my Ulric I never could be,
I vow by the saints and the blessed Marie,
Since the desolate hour when we stood by the
    shore,
And your dark galley waited to carry you o'er :
My faith then I plighted, my love I confess'd,
As I gave you the BATTLE-AXE marked with your
    crest !

* "WAPPING OLD STAIRS."

" Your Molly has never been false, she declares,
Since the last time we parted at Wapping Old Stairs ;
When I said that I would continue the same,
And gave you the 'bacco-box marked with my name.
When I passed a whole fortnight between decks with you,
Did I e'er give a kiss, Tom, to one of your crew ?
To be useful and kind to my Thomas I stay'd,
For his trousers I washed, and his grog too I made.

" Though you promised last Sunday to walk in the Mall
With Susan from Deptford and likewise with Sall,
In silence I stood your unkindness to hear,
And only upbraided my Tom with a tear.
Why should Sall, or should Susan, than me be more
    prized ?
For the heart that is true, Tom, should ne'er be despised.
Then be constant and kind, nor your Molly forsake ;
Still your trousers I'll wash, and your grog too I'll make."

When the bold barons met in my father's old hall,
Was not Edith the flower of the banquet and ball ?
In the festival hour, on the lips of your bride,
Was there ever a smile save with THEE at my
    side ?
Alone in my turret I loved to sit best,
To blazon your BANNER and broider your crest.

The knights were assembled, the tourney was
    gay !
Sir Ulric rode first in the warrior-mêlée.
In the dire battle-hour, when the tourney was
    done,
And you gave to another the wreath you had won !
Though I never reproached thee, cold. cold was
    my breast,
As I thought of that BATTLE-AXE, ah ! and that
    crest !

But away with remembrance, no more will I pine
That others usurped for a time what was mine !
There's a FESTIVAL HOUR for my Ulric and me :
Once more, as of old, shall he bend at my knee ;
Once more by the side of the knight I love best
Shall I blazon his BANNER and broider his crest.

THE ALMACK'S ADIEU.

YOUR Fanny was never false-hearted,
    And this she protests and she vows,
From the *triste moment* when we parted
    On the staircase of Devonshire House !
I blushed when you asked me to marry,
    I vowed I would never forget ;
And at parting I gave my dear Harry
    A beautiful vinegarette !

We spent *en province* all December,
  And I ne'er condescended to look
At Sir Charles, or the rich county member,
  Or even at that darling old Duke.
You were busy with dogs and with horses.
  Alone in my chamber I sat,
And made you the nicest of purses,
  And the smartest black satin cravat !

At night with that vile Lady Frances
  (*Fe faisois moi tapisserie*)
You danced every one of the dances,
  And never once thought of poor me !
Mon pauvre petit cœur ! what a shiver
  I felt as she danced the last set ;
And you gave, *O mon Dieu !* to revive her
  My beautiful vinegarette !

Return, love ! away with coquetting ;
  This flirting disgraces a man !
And ah ! all the while you're forgetting
  The heart of your poor little Fan !
Reviens ! break away from those Circes,
  Reviens, for a nice little chat ;
And I've made you the sweetest of purses,
And a lovely black satin cravat !

———

WHEN THE GLOOM IS ON THE GLEN.

When the moonlight's on the mountain
  And the gloom is on the glen,
At the cross beside the fountain
  There is one will meet thee then.
At the cross beside the fountain,
  Yes, the cross beside the fountain,
There is one will meet thee then !

I have braved, since first we met, love,
  Many a danger in my course ;
But I never can forget, love,
  That dear fountain, that old cross,
Where, her mantle shrouded o'er her—
  For the winds were chilly then—
First I met my Leonora,
  When the gloom was on the glen.

Many a clime I've ranged since then, love,
  Many a land I've wandered o'er ;
But a valley like that glen, love,
  Half so dear I never sor !
Ne'er saw maiden fairer, coyer,
  Than wert thou, my true love, when
In the gloaming first I saw yer,
  In the gloaming of the glen !

————

THE RED FLAG.

WHERE the quivering lightning flings
  His arrows from out the clouds,
And the howling tempest sings
  And whistles among the shrouds,
'Tis pleasant, 'tis pleasant to ride
  Along the foaming brine—
Wilt be the Rover's bride?
  Wilt follow him, lady mine?
              Hurrah !
For the bonny, bonny brine.

Amidst the storm and rack,
  You shall see our galley pass,
As a serpent, lithe and black,
  Glides through the waving grass.

As the vulture, swift and dark,
    Down on the ring-dove flies,
You shall see the Rover's bark
    Swoop down upon his prize.
            Hurrah !
    For the bonny, bonny prize.

Over her sides we dash,
    We gallop across her deck—
Ha ! there's a ghastly gash
    On the merchant-captain's neck—
Well shot, well shot, old Ned !
    Well struck, well struck, black James !
Our arms are red, and our foes are dead,
    And we leave a ship in flames !
            Hurrah !
    For the bonny, bonny flames !

DEAR JACK.

DEAR Jack, this white mug that with Guinness I
    fill,
And drink to the health of sweet Nan of the Hill,
Was once Tommy Tosspot's, as jovial a sot
As e'er drew a spigot, or drained a full pot—
In drinking all round 'twas his joy to surpass,
And with all merry tipplers he swigg'd off his
    glass.

One morning in summer, while seated so snug,
In the porch of his garden, discussing his jug,
Stern Death on a sudden, to Tom did appear,
And said, "Honest Thomas, come take your
    last bier."
We kneaded his clay in the shape of this can,
From which let us drink to the health of my Nan.

COMMANDERS OF THE FAITHFUL.

THE Pope he is a happy man,
His Palace is the Vatican,
And there he sits and drains his can :
The Pope he is a happy man.
I often say when I'm at home,
I'd like to be the Pope of Rome.

And then there's Sultan Saladin,
That Turkish Soldan full of sin ;
He has a hundred wives at least,
By which his pleasure is increased :
I've often wished, I hope no sin,
That I were Sultan Saladin.

But no, the Pope no wife may choose,
And so I would not wear his shoes ;
No wine may drink the proud Paynim,
And so I'd rather not be him :
My wife, my wine, I love, I hope,
And would be neither Turk, nor Pope.

———

WHEN MOONLIKE ORE THE HAZURE SEAS.

WHEN moonlike ore the hazure seas
    In soft effulgence swells,
When silver jews and balmy breaze
    Bend down the Lily's bells ;
When calm and deap, the rosy sleap
    Has lapt your soal in dreems,
R Hangeline ! R lady mine !
    Dost thou remember Jeames ?

I mark thee in the Marble All,
   Where England's loveliest shine—
I say the fairest of them hall
   Is Lady Hangeline.
My soul, in desolate eclipse,
   With recollection teems—
And then I hask, with weeping lips,
   Dost thou remember Jeames?

Away! I may not tell thee hall
   This soughring heart endures—
There is a lonely sperrit-call
   That Sorrow never cures;
There is a little, little Star,
   That still above me beams;
It is the Star of Hope—but ar!
   Dost thou remember Jeames?

KING CANUTE.

KING CANUTE was weary-hearted; he had
      reigned for years a score,
Battling, struggling, pushing, fighting, killing
      much and robbing more;
And he thought upon his actions, walking by the
      wild sea-shore.

'Twixt the Chancellor and Bishop walked the
      King with steps sedate,
Chamberlains and grooms came after, silversticks
      and goldsticks great,
Chaplains, aides-de-camp, and pages,—all the
      officers of state.

Sliding after like his shadow, pausing when he
    chose to pause,
If a frown his face contracted, straight the court-
    iers dropped their jaws ;
If to laugh the King was minded, out they burst
    in loud hee-haws.

But that day a something vexed him, that was
    clear to old and young :
Thrice his Grace had yawned at table, when his
    favorite gleemen sung,
Once the Queen would have consoled him, but
    he bade her hold her tongue.

" Something ails my gracious master," cried the
    Keeper of the Seal.
" Sure, my lord, it is the lampreys served to din-
    ner, or the veal ?"
" Psha !" exclaimed the angry monarch. " Keep-
    er, 'tis not that I feel.

" 'Tis the *heart*, and not the dinner, fool, that
    doth my rest impair :
Can a king be great as I am, prithee, and yet
    know no care ?
Oh, I'm sick, and tired, and weary."—Some one
    cried, " The King's arm-chair !"

Then towards the lackeys turning, quick my Lord
    the Keeper nodded,
Straight the King's great chair was brought him
    by two footmen able-bodied ;
Languidly he sank into it : it was comfortably
    wadded.

" Leading on my fierce companions," cried he,
    over storm and brine,

I have fought and I have conquered! Where
    was glory like to mine?"
Loudly all the courtiers echoed: "Where is
    glory like to thine?"

"What avail me all my kingdoms? Weary am
    I now and old;
Those fair sons I have begotten long to see me
    dead and cold;
Would I were, and quiet buried underneath the
    silent mould!

"Oh, remorse, the writhing serpent! at my bo-
    som tears and bites;
Horrid, horrid things I look on, though I put
    out all the lights;
Ghosts of ghastly recollections troop about my
    bed at nights.

"Cities burning, convents blazing, red with sac-
    rilegious fires;
Mothers weeping, virgins screaming vainly for
    their slaughtered sires."—
"Such a tender conscience," cries the Bishop,
    "every one admires.

"But for such unpleasant bygones cease, my
    gracious lord, to search,
They're forgotten and forgiven by our Holy
    Mother Church;
Never, never does she leave her benefactors in
    the lurch.

"Look! the land is crowned with minsters,
    which your Grace's bounty raised;
Abbeys filled with holy men, where you and
    Heaven are daily praised:

You, my lord, to think of dying ? on my conscience I'm amazed !"

" Nay, I feel," replied King Canute, "that my
end is drawing near."
" Don't say so," exclaimed the courtiers (striving
each to squeeze a tear).
" Sure your Grace is strong and lusty, and may
live this fifty year."

" Live these fifty years ?" the Bishop roared,
with actions made to suit.
" Are you mad my good Lord Keeper, thus to
speak of King Canute ?
Men have lived a thousand years, and sure his
Majesty will do't.

" Adam, Enoch, Lamech, Cainan, Mahaleel,
Methusela,
Lived nine hundred years apiece, and mayn't the
King as well as they ?"
" Fervently," exclaimed the Keeper, " Fervent-
ly I trust he may."

" *He* to die ?" resumed the Bishop. " He a
mortal like to *us ?*
Death was not for him intended, though *commu-
nis omnibus :*
Keeper, you are irreligious for to talk and cavil
thus.

" With his wondrous skill in healing ne'er a doc-
can compete,
Loathsome lepers, if he touch them, start up clean
upon their feet ;
Surely he could raise the dead up, did his High-
ness think it meet.

"Did not once the Jewish captain stay the sun
    upon the hill,
And, the while he slew the foemen, bid the silver
    moon stand still ?
So, no doubt, could gracious Canute, if it were
    his sacred will."

"Might I stay the sun above us, good Sir Bish-
    op ?" Canute cried ;
"Could I bid the silver moon to pause upon her
    heavenly ride ?
If the moon obeys my orders, sure I can com-
    mand the tide.

"Will the advancing waves obey me, Bishop, if
    I make the sign ?"
Said the Bishop, bowing lowly, "Land and sea,
    my lord, are thine."
Canute turned towards the ocean—"Back !" he
    said, "thou foaming brine.

"From the sacred shore I stand on, I command
    thee to retreat ;
Venture not, thou stormy rebel, to approach thy
    master's seat :
Ocean, be thou still ! I bid thee come not nearer
    to my feet !"

But the sullen ocean answered with a louder,
    deeper roar,
And the rapid waves drew nearer, falling sound-
    ing on the shore ;
Back the Keeper and the Bishop, back the King
    and courtiers bore.

And he sternly bade them never more to kneel to
    human clay,

But alone to praise and worship That which earth
    and seas obey :
And his golden crown of empire never wore he
    from that day.
King Canute is dead and gone : Parasites exist
    alway.

————

FRIAR'S SONG.

SOME love the matin-chimes, which tell
    The hour of prayer to sinner :
But better far's the mid-day bell,
    Which speaks the hour of dinner ;
For when I see a smoking fish,
    Or capon drown'd in gravy,
Or noble haunch on silver dish,
    Full glad I sing my ave.

My pulpit is an alehouse bench,
    Whereon I sit so jolly ;
A smiling rosy country wench
    My saint and patron holy.
I kiss her cheek so red and sleek,
    I press her ringlets wavy,
And in her willing ear I speak
    A most religious ave.

And if I'm blind, yet Heaven is kind,
    And holy saints forgiving ;
For sure he leads a right good life
    Who thus admires good living.
Above, they say, our flesh is air,
    Our blood celestial ichor :
Oh, grant ! 'mid all the changes there,
    They may not change our liquor !

ATRA CURA.

BEFORE I lost my five poor wits,
I mind me of a Romish clerk,
Who sang how Care, the phantom dark,
Beside the belted horseman sits.
Methought I saw the grisly sprite
Jump up but now behind my Knight.

And though he gallop as he may,
I mark that cursed monster black
Still sits behind his honor's back,
Tight squeezing of his heart alway.
Like two black Templars sit they there,
Beside one crupper, Knight and Care.

No knight am I with pennoned spear,
To prance upon a bold destrere :
I will not have black Care prevail
Upon my long-eared charger's tail ;
For lo, I am a witless fool,
And laugh at Grief and ride a mule.

———

REQUIESCAT.

UNDER the stone you behold,
Buried, and coffined, and cold,
Lieth Sir Wilfrid the Bold.

Always he marched in advance,
Warring in Flanders and France,
Doughtly with sword and with lance.

Famous in Saracen fight,
Rode in his youth the good knight,
Scattering Paynims in flight.

Brian, the Templar untrue,
Fairly in tourney he slew,
Saw Hierusalem too.

Now he is buried and gone,
Lying beneath the gray stone :
Where shall you find such a one ?

Long time his widow deplored,
Weeping the fate of her lord,
Sadly cut off by the sword.

When she was eased of her pain,
Came the good Lord Athelstane,
When her ladyship married again

———

THE WILLOW-TREE.

KNOW ye the willow-tree
   Whose gray leaves quiver,
Whispering gloomily
   To yon pale river?
Lady, at even-tide
   Wander not near it :
They say its branches hide
   A sad, lost spirit !

Once to the willow-tree
   A maid came fearful ;
Pale seemed her cheek to be,
   Her blue eye tearful.

Soon as she saw the tree,
  Her step moved fleeter ;
No one was there—ah me !
  No one to meet her !

Quick beat her heart to hear
  The far bells' chime
Toll from the chapel-tower
  The trysting time :
But the red sun went down
  In golden flame,
And though she looked round,
  Yet no one came !

Presently came the night,
  Sadly to greet her,—
Moon in her silver light,
  Stars in their glitter ;
Then sank the moon away
  Under the billow,
Still wept the maid alone—
  There by the willow !

Through the long darkness,
  By the stream rolling,
Hour after hour went on
  Tolling and tolling.
Long was the darkness,
  Lonely and stilly ;
Shrill came the night-wind,
  Piercing and chilly.

Shrill blew the morning breeze,
  Biting and cold,
Bleak peers the gray dawn
  Over the wold.

Bleak over moor and stream
  Looks the gray dawn,
Gray, with dishevelled hair,
Still stands the willow there—
  THE MAID IS GONE !

Domine, Domine !
* Sing we a litany,—*
Sing for the poor maiden-hearts broken and weary;
Domine, Domine !
* Sing we a litany,*
Wail we and weep we a wild Miserere !

———

THE WILLOW-TREE.

(ANOTHER VERSION.)

I.

LONG by the willow-tree
  Vainly they sought her,
Wild rang the mother's screams
  O'er the gray water :
" Where is my lovely one ?
  Where is my daughter ?

II.

" Rouse thee, sir constable—
  Rouse thee and look ;
Fisherman, bring your net,
  Boatman your hook.
Beat in the lily-beds,
  Dive in the brook !"

III.

Vainly the constable
    Shouted and called her ;
Vainly the fisherman
    Beat the green alder,
Vainly he flung the net,
    Never it hauled her !

IV.

Mother beside the fire
    Sat, her nightcap in ;
Father, in easy chair,
    Gloomily napping,
When at the window-sill
    Came a light tapping !

V.

And a pale countenance
    Looked through the casement.
Loud beat the mother's heart
    Sick with amazement,
And at the vision which
    Came to surprise her,
Shrieked in an agony—
    " Lor ! it's Elizar !"

VI.

Yes, 'twas Elizabeth—
    Yes, 'twas their girl ;
Pale was her cheek, and her
    Hair out of curl.
" Mother !" the loving one,
    Blushing, exclaimed,
" Let not your innocent
    Lizzy be blamed.

VII.

" Yesterday, going to aunt
    Jones's to tea,
Mother, dear mother, I
    Forgot the door-key !
And as the night was cold,
    And the way steep,
Mrs. Jones kept me to
    Breakfast and sleep."

VIII.

Whether her Pa and Ma
    Fully believed her,
That we shall never know,
    Stern they received her ;
And for the work of that
    Cruel, though short, night,
Sent her to bed without
    Tea for a fortnight.

IX.

MORAL.

Hey diddle diddlety,
Cat and the Fiddlety,
Maidens of England, take caution by she !
Let love and suicide
Never tempt you aside,
And always remember to take the door-key.

LYRA HIBERNICA.

THE POEMS OF THE MOLONY OF KILBALLYMOLONY.

THE PIMLICO PAVILION.

YE pathrons of Janius, Minerva and Vanius,
  Who sit on Parnassus, that mountain of snow,
Descind from your station and make observation
  Of the Prince's pavilion in sweet Pimlico.

This garden, by jakurs, is forty poor acres,
  (The garner he tould me, and sure ought to
    know ;)
And yet greatly bigger, in size and in figure,
  Than the Phanix itself, seems the Park Pimlico.

O 'tis there that the spoort is, when the Queen
    and the Coort is
  Walking magnanimous all of a row,
Forgetful what state is among the patatics
  And the pineapple gardens of sweet Pimlico.

There in blossoms odorous the birds sing a
    chorus
  Of " God save the Queen" as they hop to and
    fro ;

And you sit on the binches and hark to the
　finches,
　Singing melodious in sweet Pimlico.

There shuiting their phanthasies, they pluck poly-
　anthuses
　That round in the gardens resplindently grow,
Wid roses and jessimins, and other sweet speci-
　mins,
　Would charm bould Linnayus in sweet Pimlico.

You see when you inther, and stand in the cin-
　ther,
　Where the roses, and necturns, and collyflow-
　ers blow,
A hill so tremindous, it tops the top-windows
　Of the elegant houses of famed Pimlico.

And when you've ascinded that precipice splindid
　You see on its summit a wondtherful show—
A lovely Swish building, all painting and gilding,
　The famous Pavilion of sweet Pimlico.

Prince Albert, of Flandthers, that Prince of Com-
　mandthers,
　(On whom my best blessings hereby I bestow,)
With goold and vermilion has decked that Pavil-
　ion,
　Where the Queen may take tay in her sweet
　Pimlico.

There's lines from John Milton the chamber all
　gilt on,
　And pictures beneath them that's shaped like
　a bow ;
I was greatly astounded to think that that Round-
　head
　Should find an admission to famed Pimlico.

O lovely's each fresco, and most picturesque O ;
  And while round the chamber astonished I go,
I think Dan Maclise's it baits all the pieces
  Surrounding the cottage of famed Pimlico.

Eastlake has the chimney, (a good one to limn he,)
  And a vargin he paints with a sarpent below ;
While bulls, pigs, and panthers, and other en-
    chanthers,
  Are painted by Landseer in sweet Pimlico.

And nature smiles opposite. Stanfield he copies it ;
  O'er Claude or Poussang sure 'tis he that may
    crow :
But Sir Ross's best faiture is small miniáture—
  He shouldn't paint fresçoes in famed Pimlico.

There's Leslie and Uwins has rather small
    doings ;
  There's Dyce, as brave masther as England
    can show ;
And the flowers and the sthrawberries, sure he
    no dauber is,
  That painted the panels of famed Pimlico.

In the pictures from Walther Scott, never a fault
    there's got,
  Sure the marble's as natural as thrue Scaglio ;
And the Chamber Pompayen is sweet to take tay
    in,
  And ait butther'd muffins in sweet Pimlico.

There's landscapes by Gruner, both solar and
    lunar,
  Them two little Doyles, too, deserve a bravo ;
Wid de piece by young Townsend, (for janius
    abounds in't ;)
  And that's why he's shuited to paint Pimlico.

That picture of Severn's is worthy of rever'nce
But some I won't mintion is rather so so ;
For sweet philosóphy, or crumpets and coffee,
O where's a Pavilion like sweet Pimlico ?

O to praise this Pavilion would puzzle Quintilian,
Daymosthenes, Brougham, or young Cicero :
So, heavenly Goddess, d'ye pardon my modesty,
And silence, my lyre ! about sweet Pimlico.

THE CRYSTAL PALACE.

WITH janial foire
Transfuse me loyre,
Ye sacred nymphs of Pindus,
The whoile I sing
That wondthrous thing,
The Palace made o' windows !

Say, Paxton, truth,
Thou wondthrous youth,
What sthroke of art celistial,
What power was lint
You to invint
This combineetion cristial.

O would before
That Thomas Moore,
Likewoise the late Lord Boyron,
Thim aigles sthrong
Of godlike song,
Cast oi on that cast oiron !

And saw thim walls,
And glittering halls,
Thim rising slendther columns

Which I, poor pote,
Could not denote,
No, not in twinty vollums.

My Muse's words
Is like the bird's
That roosts beneath the panes there ;
Her wings she spoils
'Gainst them bright toiles,
And cracks her silly brains there.

This Palace tall,
This Cristial Hall,
Which Imperors might covet,
Stands in High Park
Like Noah's Ark,
A rainbow bint above it.

The towers and fanes,
In other scaynes,
The fame of this will undo,
Saint Paul's big doom,
Saint Payther's Room,
And Dublin's proud Rotundo.

'Tis here that roams,
As well becomes
Her dignitee and stations,
Victoria Great,
And houlds in state
The Congress of the Nations.

Her subjects pours
From distant shores,
Her Injians and Canajians ;
And also we,
Her kingdoms three,
Attind with our allagiance.

Here come likewise
Her bould allies,
Both Asian and Europian ;
From East and West
They send their best
To fill her Coornucopean.

I seen (thank Grace !)
This wondthrous place
(His Noble Honor Misther
H. Cole it was
That gave the pass,
And let me see what is there).

With conscious proide
I stud insoide
And look'd the World's Great Fair in,
Until me sight
Was dazzled quite,
And couldn't see for staring.

There's holy saints
And window paints,
By Maydiayval Pugin ;
Alhamborough Jones
Did paint the tones
Of yellow and gambouge in.

There's fountains there
And crosses fair ;
There's water-gods with urrns :
There's organs three,
To play d'ye see ?
" God save the Queen," by turrns.

There's statues bright
Of marble white,
Of silver, and of copper ;

And some in zinc,
And some, I think,
That isn't over proper.

There's staym ingynes,
That stands in lines,
Enormous and amazing,
That squeal and snort
Like whales in sport,
Or elephants a-grazing.

There's carts and gigs,
And pins for pigs,
There's dibblers and there's harrows,
And ploughs like toys
For little boys,
And ilegant wheelbarrows.

For thim genteels
Who ride on wheels,
There's plenty to indulge 'em :
There's droskys snug
From Paytersbug,
And vayhycles from Bulgium.

There's cabs on stands
And shandthry danns ;
There's waggons from New York here ;
There's Lapland sleighs
Have cross'd the seas,
And jaunting cyars from Cork here.

Amazed I pass
From glass to glass,
Deloighted I survey 'em ;
Fresh wondthers grows
Before me nose
In this sublime Musayum !

Look, here's a fan
From far Japan,
A sabre from Damasco :
   There's shawls ye get
   From far Thibet,
And cotton prints from Glasgow.

   There's German flutes,
   Marocky boots,
And Naples macaronies ;
   Bohaymia
   Has sent Bohay ;
Polonia her polonies.

   There's granite flints
   That's quite imminse,
There's sacks of coals and fuels,
   There's swords and guns,
   And soap in tuns,
And gingerbread and jewels.

   There's taypots there,
   And cannons rare ;
There's coffins fill'd with roses ;
   There's canvas tints,
   Teeth insthrumints,
And shuits of clothes by MOSES.

   There's lashins more
   Of things in store,
But thim I don't remimber ;
   Nor could disclose
   Did I compose
From May time to Novimber !

   Ah, JUDY thru !
   With eyes so blue,
That you were here to view it !

And could I screw
But tu pound tu,
'Tis I would thrait you to it !

So let us raise
Victoria's praise,
And Albert's proud condition,
That takes his ayse
As he surveys
This Cristial Exhibition.

MOLONY'S LAMENT.

O Tim, did you hear of thim Saxons,
   And read what the peepers report ?
They're goan to recal the Liftinant,
   And shut up the Castle and Coort !
Our desolate counthry of Oireland
   They're bint, the blagyards, to desthroy,
And now having murdthered our counthry,
   They're goin to kill the Viceroy,
      Dear boy ;
   'Twas he was our proide and our joy !

And will we no longer behould him,
   Surrounding his carriage in throngs,
As he waves his cocked-hat from the windies,
   And smiles to his bould aid-de-congs ?
I liked for to see the young haroes,
   All shoining with sthripes and with stars,
A horsing about in the Phaynix,
   And winking the girls in the cyars,
      Like Mars,
   A smokin' their poipes and cigyars.

Dear Mitchell exoiled to Bermudies,
  Your beautiful oilids you'll ope,
And there'll be an abondance of croyin'
  From O'Brine at the Keep of Good Hope,
When they read of this news in the peepers,
  Acrass the Atlantical wave,
That the last of the Oirish Liftinints
  Of the oisland of Seents has tuck lave.
          God save
  The Queen—she should betther behave.

And what's to become of poor Dame Sthreet,
  And who'll ait the puffs and the tarts,
Whin the Coort of imparial splindor
  From Doblin's sad city departs?
And who'll have the fiddlers and pipers,
  When the deuce of a Coort there remains?
And where'll be the bucks and the ladies,
  To hire the Coort-shuits and the thrains?
          In sthrains,
  It's thus that ould Erin complains!

There's Counsellor Flanagan's leedy,
  'Twas she in the Coort didn't fail,
And she wanted a plinty of popplin,
  For her dthress, and her flounce, and her tail;
She bought it of Misthress O' Grady,
  Eight shillings a yard tabinet,
But now that the Coort is concluded,
  The divvle a yard will she get;
          I bet,
  Bedad, that she wears the ould set

There's Surgeon O'Toole and Miss Leary,
  They'd daylings at Madam O'Riggs';
Each year at the dthrawing-room sayson,
  They mounted the neatest of wigs.

When Spring, with its buds and its daisies,
  Comes out in her beauty and bloom,
Thim tu'll never think of new jasies,
  Because there is is no dthrawing-room,
     For whom
They'd choose the expense to ashume.

There's Alderman Toad and his lady,
  'Twas they gave the Clart and the Poort,
And the poineapples, turbots, and lobsters,
  To feast the Lord Liftinint's Coort.
But now that the quality's goin,
  I warnt that the aiting will stop,
And you'll get at the Alderman's teeble
  The devil a bite or a dthrop,
     Or chop ;
And the butcher may shut up his shop.

Yes, the grooms and the ushers are goin,
  And his Lordship, the dear honest man,
And the Duchess, his eemiable leedy,
  And Corry, the bould Connellan,
And little Lord Hyde and the childthren,
  And the Chewter and Governess tu ;
And the servants are packing their boxes,—
  Oh, murther, but what shall I due
     Without you ?
O Meery, with ois of the blue !

MR. MOLONY'S ACCOUNT OF THE BALL

GIVEN TO THE NEPAULESE AMBASSADOR BY THE PENIN-
SULAR AND ORIENTAL COMPANY.

O WILL ye choose to hear the news,
   Bedad I cannot pass it o'er :
I'll tell you all about the Ball
   To the Naypaulase Ambassador.
Begor ! this fête all balls does bate
   At which I've worn a pump, and I
Must here relate the splendthor great
   Of th' Oriental Company.

These men of sinse dispoised expinse,
   To fête these black Achilleses.
" We'll show the blacks," says they, "Almack's,"
   " And take the rooms at Willis's."
With flags and shawls, for these Nepauls,
   They hung the rooms of Willis up,
And decked the walls, and stairs, and hails,
   With roses and with lilies up.

And Jullien's band it tuck its stand
   So sweetly in the middle there,
And soft bassoons played heavenly chunes,
   And violins did fiddle there.
And when the Coort was tired of spoort,
   I'd lave you, boys, to think there was
A nate buffet before them set,
   Where lashins of good dhrink there was.

At ten before the ball-room door,
   His moighty Excelléncy was,
He smoiled and bowed to all the crowd,
   So gorgeous and immense he was.

His dusky shuit, sublime and mute,
  Into the door-way followed him ;
And O the noise of the blackguard boys,
  As they hurrood and hollowed him !

The noble Chair * stud at the stair,
  And bade the dthrums to thump ; and he
Did thus evince, to that Black Prince,
  The welcome of his Company.
O fair the girls, and rich the curls,
  And bright the oys you saw there, was ;
And fixed each oye, ye there could spoi,
  On Gineral Jung Bahawther, was !

This Gineral great then tuck his sate,
  With all the other ginerals,
(Bedad his troat, his belt, his coat,
  All bleezed with precious minerals ;)
And as he there, with princely air
  Recloinin on his cushion was,
All round about his royal chair
  The squeezin and the pushin was.

O Pat, such girls, such Jukes, and Earls,
  Such fashion and nobilitee !
Just think of Tim, and fancy him
  Amidst the hoigh gentilitee !
There was Lord De L'Huys, and the Portygeese
  Ministher and his lady there,
And I reckonised, with much surprise,
  Our messmate, Bob O'Grady, there ;

* James Matheson, Esq., to whom, and the Board of
Directors of the Peninsular and Oriental Company, I,
Timotheus Molony, late stoker on board the " Iberia,"
the " Lady Mary Wood," the " Tagus," and the Oriental
steamships, humbly dedicate this production of my grateful muse.

There was Baroness Brunow, that looked like Juno,
    And Baroness Rehausen there,
And Countess Roullier, that looked peculiar
    Well, in her robes of gauze in there.
There was Lord Crowhurst (I knew him first,
    When only Mr. Pips he was),
And Mick O'Toole, the great big fool,
    That after supper tipsy was.

There was Lord Fingall, and his ladies all,
    And Lords Killeen and Dufferin,
And Paddy Fife, with his fat wife ;
    I wondther how he could stuff her in.
There was Lord Belfast, that by me past,
    And seemed to ask how should *I* go there ?
And the Widow Macrae, and Lord A. Hay,
    And the Marchioness of Sligo there.

Yes, Jukes, and Earls, and diamonds, and pearls,
    And pretty girls, was spoorting there ;
And some beside (the rogues !) I spied,
    Behind the windies, coorting there.
Oh, there's one I know, bedad, would show
    As beautiful as any there,
And I'd like to hear the pipers blow,
    And shake a fut with Fanny there !

THE BATTLE OF LIMERICK.

YE Genii of the nation,
    Who look with veneration,
And Ireland's desolation onsaysingly deplore
    Ye sons of General Jackson,
    Who thrample on the Saxon,
Attend to the thransaction upon Shannon shore.

When William, Duke of Schumbug,
A tyrant and a humbug,
With cannon and with thunder on our city bore,
Our fortitude and valliance
Insthructed his battalions
To rispict the galliant Irish upon Shannon shore.

Since that capitulation,
No city in this nation
So grand a reputation could boast before,
As Limerick prodigious,
That stands with quays and bridges,
And the ships up to the windies of the Shannon
shore.

A chief of ancient line,
'Tis William Smith O'Brine
Reprisints this darling Limerick, this ten years or
more :
O the Saxons can't endure
To see him on the flure,
And thrimble at the Cicero from Shannon shore !

This valliant son of Mars
Had been to visit Par's,
That land of Revolution, that grows the tricolor ;
And to welcome his returrn
From pilgrimages furren,
We invited him to tay on the Shannon shore.

Then we summoned to our board
Young Meagher of the sword ;
'Tis he will sheathe that battle-axe in Saxon gore ;
And Mitchil of Belfast
We bade to our repast,
To dthrink a dish of coffee on the Shannon shore.

Convaniently to hould
These patriots so bould,
We tuck the opportunity of Tim Doolan's store :
And with ornamints and banners
(As becomes gintale good manners)
We made the loveliest tay-room upon Shannon
shore.

'Twould binifit your sowls
To see the buttherd rowls,
The sugar-tongs and sangwidges and craim gal-
yore,
And the muffins and the crumpets,
And the band of harps and thrumpets,
To celebrate the sworry upon Shannon shore.

Sure the Imperor of Rohay
Would be proud to dthrink the tay
That Misthress Biddy Rooney for O'Brine did
pour ;
And since the days of Strongbow,
There never was such Congo—
Mitchil dthrank six quarts of it—by Shannon shore.

But Clarndon and Corry
Connellan beheld this sworry
With rage and imulation in their black hearts' core ;
And they hired a gang of ruffins
To interrupt the muffins
And the fragrance of the Congo on the Shannon
shore.

When full of tay and cake,
O'Brine began to spake ;
But juice a one could hear him, for a sudden roar
Of a ragamuffin rout
Began to yell and shout,
And frighten the propriety of Shannon shore.

As Smith O'Brine harangued,
They batthered and they banged :
Tim Doolan's doors and windies down they tore ;
They smashed the lovely windies
(Hung with muslin from the Indies),
'urshuing of their shindies upon Shannon shore.

With throwing of brickbats,
Drowned puppies and dead rats,
These ruffin democrats themselves did lower ;
Tin kettles, rotten eggs,
Cabbage-stalks, and wooden legs,
They flung among the patriots of Shannon shore.

O the girls began to scrame
And upset the milk and crame ;
And the honorable gintlemin, they cursed and
    swore :
And Mitchil of Belfast,
'Twas he that looked aghast,
When they roasted him in effigy by Shannon shore.

O the lovely tay was spilt
On that day of Ireland's guilt ;
Says Jack Mitchil, " I am kilt ! Boys, where's the
    back door ?
'Tis a national disgrace :
Let me go and veil me face ;"
And he boulted with quick pace from the Shannon
    shore.

" Cut down the bloody horde !"
Says Meagher of the sword,
" This conduct would disgrace any blackamore ;"
But the best use Tommy made
Of his famous battle blade
Was to cut his own stick from the Shannon shore.

Immortal Smith O'Brine
Was raging like a line ;
'Twould have done your sowl good to have heard
    him roar ;
In his glory he arose,
And he rush'd upon his foes,
But they hit him on the nose by the Shannon shore.

Then the Futt and the Dthragoons
In squadthrons and platoons,
With their music playing chunes, down upon us
    bore ;
And they bate the rattatoo,
But the Peelers came in view,
And ended the shaloo on the Shannon shore.

LARRY O'TOOLE.

You've all heard of Larry O'Toole,
Of the beautiful town of Drumgoole ;
    He had but one eye,
    To ogle ye by—
Oh, murther, but that was a jew'l !
    A fool
He made of de girls, dis O'Toole.

'Twas he was the boy didn't fail,
That tuck down pataties and mail ;
    He never would shrink
    From any strong dthrink,
Was it whiskey or Drogheda ale ;
    I'm bail
This Larry would swallow a pail.

Oh, many a night at the bowl,
With Larry I've sot cheek by jowl ;
    He's gone to his rest,
    Where there's dthrink of the best,
And so let us give his old sowl
    A howl,
For t'was he made the noggin to rowl.

THE ROSE OF FLORA.

SENT BY A YOUNG GENTLEMAN OF QUALITY TO MISS BR-DY,
OF CASTLE BRADY.

ON Brady's towers there grows a flower,
    It is the loveliest flower that blows,—
At Castle Brady there lives a lady
    (And how I love her no one knows) ;
Her name is Nora, and the goddess Flora
    Presents her with this blooming rose.

"O Lady Nora,"says the goddess Flora,
    " I've many a rich and bright parterre ;
In Brady's towers there's seven more flowers,
    But you're the fairest lady there :
Not all the county, nor Ireland's bounty,
    Can projuice a treasure that's half so fair !"

What cheek is redder ? sure roses fed her !
    Her hair is maregolds, and her eyes of blew.
Beneath her eyelid, is like the vi'let,
    That darkly glistens with gentle jew !
The lily's nature is not surely whiter
    Than Nora's neck is,—and her arrums too.

"Come, gentle Nora," says the goddess Flora,
 " My dearest creature, take my advice :
There is a poet, full well you know it,
 Who spends his lifetime in heavy sighs,—
Young Redmond Barry, 'tis him you'll marry,
 If rhyme and raisin you'd choose likewise."

THE LAST IRISH GRIEVANCE.

On reading of the general indignation occasioned
in Ireland by the appointment of a Scotch Professor to one of HER MAJESTY'S Godless Colleges,
MASTER MOLLOY MOLONY, brother of THADDEUS
MOLONY, ESQ., of the Temple, a youth only fifteen years of age, dashed off the following spirited
lines :

As I think of the insult that's done to this nation,
 Red tears of rivinge from me faytures I wash,
And uphold in this pome, to the world's daytista-
 tion,
 The sleeves that appointed PROFESSOR M'COSH.

I look round me counthree, renowned by expari-
 ence,
 And see midst her childthren, the witty, the
 wise,—
Whole hayps of logicians, poets, schollars, gram-
 marians,
 All ayger for pleeces, all panting to rise ;

I gaze round the world in its utmost diminsion ;
 LARD JAHN and his minions in Council I ask,
Was there ever a Government-pleece (with a pinsion)
 But the children of Erin were fit for that task ?

What, Erin beloved, is thy fetal condition?
  What shame in aych boosom must rankle and
    burrun,
To think that our countree has ne'er a logician
  In the hour of her deenger will surrev her turrun!

On the logic of Saxons there's little reliance,
  And, rather from Saxon than gather its rules,
I'd stamp under feet the base book of his science,
  And spit on his chair as he taught in the schools!

O false SIR JOHN KANE! is it thus that you praych
  me?
  I think all your Queen's Universitees Bosh;
And if you've no nective Professor to taych me,
  I scawurn to be learned by the Saxon M'Cosh.

There's WISEMAN and CHUME, and His Grace the
  Lord Primate,
  That sinds round the box, and the world will
    subscribe:
'Tis they'll build a College that's fit for our cli-
  mate,
  And taych me the saycrets I burn to imboibe!

'Tis there as a Student of Science I'll enther,
  Fair Fountain of Knowledge, of Joy, and
    Contint!
SAINT PATHRICK's sweet Statue shall stand in the
  centher,
  And wink his dear oi every day during Lint.

And good DOCTOR NEWMAN, that praycher unwary,
  'Tis he shall preside the Academee School,
And quit the gay robe of ST. PHILIP of Neri,
  To wield the soft rod of ST. LAWRENCE
    O'TOOLE!

THE

BALLADS OF POLICEMAN X.

THE WOFLE NEW BALLAD OF JANE RONEY AND MARY BROWN.

AN igstrawnary tail I vill tell you this veek—
I stood in the Court of A'Beckett the Beak,
Vere Mrs. Jane Roney, a vidow, I see,
Who charged Mary Brown with a robbin of she.

This Mary was pore and in misery once,
And she came to Mrs. Roney it's more than
    twelve monce.
She adn't got no bed, nor no dinner nor no tea,
And kind Mrs. Roney gave Mary all three.

Mrs. Roney kep Mary for ever so many vecks,
(Her conduct disgusted the best of all Beax,)
She kep her for nothink, as kind as could be,
Never thinkin that this Mary was a traitor to
    she.

"Mrs. Roney, O Mrs. Roney, I feel very ill ;
Will you just step to the Doctor's for to fetch me
    a pill?"
"That I will, my pore Mary," Mrs. Roney says
    she ;
And she goes off to the Doctor's as quickly as
    may be.

No sooner on this message Mrs. Roney was sped,
Than hup gits vicked Mary, and jumps out a
    bed ;
She hopens all the trunks without never a key—
She bustes all the boxes, and vith them makes
    free.

Mrs. Roney's best linning, gownds, petticoats,
    and close,
Her children's little coats and things, her boots,
    and her hose,
She packed them, and she stole 'em, and avay
    vith them did flee.
Mrs. Roney's situation—you may think vat it
    vould be !

Of Mary, ungrateful, who had served her this
    vay,
Mrs. Roney heard nothink for a long year and a
    day.
Till last Thursday, in Lambeth, ven whom should
    she see
But this Mary, as had acted so ungrateful to
    she ?

She was leaning on the helbo of a worthy young
    man,
They were going to be married, and were walkin
    hand in hand ;
And the Church bells was a ringing for Mary and
    he,
And the parson was ready, and a waitin for his
    fee.

When up comes Mrs. Roney, and faces Mary
    Brown,
Who trembles, and castes her eyes upon the
    ground.

She calls a jolly pleaseman, it happens to be me ;
I charge this young woman, Mr. Pleaseman, says
    she.   .

" Mrs. Roney, o, Mrs. Roney, o, do let me go.
I acted most ungrateful I own, and I know,
But the marriage bell is a ringin, and the ring
    you may see,
And this young man is a waitin," says Mary says
    she.

" I don't care three fardens for the parson and
    clark,
And the bell may keep ringin from noonday to
    dark.
Mary Brown, Mary Brown, you must come along
    with me ;
And I think this young man is lucky to be free."

So, in spite of the tears which bejew'd Mary's
    cheek,
I took that young gurl to A'Beckett the Beak ;
That exlent Justice demanded her plea—
But never a sullable said Mary said she.

On account of her conduck so base and so vile,
That wicked young gurl is committed for trile,
And if she's transpawted beyond the salt sea,
It's a proper reward for such willians as she.

Now you young gurls of Southwark for Mary
    who veep,
From pickin and stealin your ands you must
    keep,
Or it may be my dooty, as it was Thursday veek,
To pull you all hup to A'Beckett the Beak.

THE THREE CHRISTMAS WAITS.

My name is Pleaceman X ;
   Last night I was in bed,
A dream did me perplex,
   Which came into my Edd.
I dreamed I sor three Waits
   A playing of their tune,
At Pimlico Palace gates,
   All underneath the moon.
One puffed a hold French horn,
   And one a hold Banjo,
And one chap seedy and torn
   A Hirish pipe did blow.
They sadly piped and played,
   Dexcribing of their fates ;
And this was what they said,
   Those three pore Christmas waits :—

" When this black year began,
   This Eighteen-forty-eight,
I was a great great man,
   And king both vise and great,
And Munseer Guizot by me did show
   As Minister of State.

" But Febuwerry came,
   And brought a rabble rout,
And me and my good dame
   And children did turn out,
And us, in spite of all our right,
   Sent to the right about.

" I left my native ground,
   I left my kin and kith,
I left my royal crownd,
   Vich I couldn't travel vith,

And without a pound came to English ground
  In the name of Mr. Smith.

" Like any anchorite
  I've lived since I came here,
I've kep myself quite quite,
  I've drank the small small beer,
And the vater, you see, disagrees vith me
  And all my famly dear.

" O Tweeleries so dear,
  O darling Pally Royl,
Vas it to finish here
  That I did trouble and toyl ?
That all my plans should break in my ands,
  And should on me recoil ?

" My state I fenced about
  Vith baynicks and vith guns ;
My gals I portioned hout,
  Rich vives I got my sons ;
O varn't it crule to lose my rule,
  My money and lands at once ?

" And so, vid arp and woice,
  Both troubled and shagreened,
I bid you to rejoice,
  O glorious England's Queend !
And never have to veep, like pore Louis-Phileep
  Because you out are cleaned.

" O Prins, so brave and stout,
  I stand before your gate ;
Pray send a trifle hout
  To me, your pore old Vait ;
For nothink could be vuss than it's been along
      vith us
  In this year Forty-eight."

" Ven this bad year began,"
   The next man said, saysee,
" I vas a Journeyman,
   A taylor black and free,
And my wife went out and chaired about,
   And my name's the bold Cuffee.

" The Queen and Halbert both
   I swore I would confound,
I took a hawfle hoath
   To drag them to the ground ;
And sevral more with me they swore
   Aginst the British Crownd.

" Aginst her Pleaceman all
   We said we'd try our strenth ;
Her scarlick soldiers tall
   We vow'd we'd lay full lenth :
And out we came, in Freedom's name,
   Last Aypril was the tenth.

" Three 'undred thousand snobs
   Came out to stop the vay,
Vith sticks vith iron knobs,
   Or else we'd gained the day.
The harmy quite kept out of sight,
   And so ve vent avay.

" Next day the Pleacemen came—
   Rewenge it was their plann—
And from my good old dame
   They took her tailor-mann :
And the hard hard beak did me bespeak
   To Newgit in the Wann.

" In that etrocious Cort
   The Jewry did agree ;

The Judge did me transport,
  To go beyond the sea :
And so for life, from his dear wife
  They took poor old Cuffee.

" O Halbert, Appy Prince ?
  With children round your knees,
Ingraving ansum Prints,
  And taking hoff your hease ;
O think of me, the old Cuffee,
  Beyond the solt solt seas !

" Although I'm hold and black,
  My hanguish is most great ;
Great Prince, O call me back,
  And I vill be your Vait !
And never no more vill break the Lor,
  As I did in 'Forty-eight,"

The tailer thus did close
  (A pore old blackymore rogue),
When a dismal gent uprose,
  And spoke with Hirish brogue :
" I'm Smith O'Brine, of Royal Line
  Descended from Rory Ogue.

" When great O'Connle died,
  That man whom all did trust,
That man whom Henglish pride
  Beheld with such disgust,
Then Erin free fixed eyes on me,
  And swoar I should be fust.

" ' The glorious Hirish Crown,'
  Says she, ' it shall be thine :
Long time, it's wery well known
  You kep it in your line ;
That diadem of hemerald gem
  Is yours, my Smith O'Brine.

" ' Too long the Saxon churl
 Our land encumbered hath ;
Arise, my Prince, my Earl,
 And brush them from thy path :
Rise, mighty Smith, and sweep 'em vith
 The besom of your wrath.'

" Then in my might I rose,
 My country I surveyed,
I saw it filled with foes,
 I viewed them undismayed ;
' Ha, ha !' says I, ' the harvest's high,
 I'll reap it with my blade.'

" My warriors I enrolled,
 They rallied round their lord ;
And cheafs in council old
 I summond to the board—
Wise Doheny and Duffy bold,
 And Meagher of the Sword.

" I stood on Slievenamaun,
 They came with pikes and bills ;
They gathered in the dawn,
 Like mist upon the hills,
And rushed adown the mountain side
Like twenty thousand rills.

" Their fortress we assail ;
 Hurroo ! my boys, hurroo !
The bloody Saxons quail
 To hear the wild shaloo :
Strike, and prevail, proud Innesfail,
 O'Brine aboo, aboo !

" Our people they defied ;
 They shot at 'em like savages,
Their bloody guns they plied
 With sanguinary ravages :

Hide, blushing Glory, hide
That day among the cabbages !

" And so no more I'll say,
But ask your Mussy great,
And humbly sing and pray,
Your Majesty's poor Wait :
Your Smith O'Brine in 'Forty-nine
Will blush for 'Forty-eight."

LINES ON A LATE HOSPICIOUS EWENT.*

BY A GENTLEMAN OF THE FOOT-GUARDS (BLUE).

I PACED upon my beat
With steady step and slow,
All huppandownd of Ranelagh Street ;
Ran'lagh St. Pimlico.

While marching huppandownd
Upon that fair May morn,
Beold the booming cannings sound,
A royal child is born !

The Ministers of State
Then presenly I sor,
They gallops to the Pallis gate,
In carridges and for.

With anxious looks intent,
Before the gate they stop,
There comes the good Lord President,
And there the Archbishopp.

* The birth of Prince Arthur.

Lord John he next elights ;
   And who comes here in haste ?
'Tis the ero of one underd fights,
   The caudle for to taste.

Then Mrs. Lily, the nuss,
   Towards them steps with joy :
Says the brave old Duke, "Come tell to us,
   Is it a gal or a boy ?"

Says Mrs. L. to the Duke,
   " Your Grace, it is *a Prince.*"
And at that nuss's bold rebuke
   He did both laugh and wince.

He vews with pleasant look
   This pooty flower of May,
Then says the wenerable Duke,
   " Egad, it's my buthday,"

By memory backards borne,
   Peraps his thoughts did stray
To that old place where he was born
   Upon the first of May.

Perhaps he did recall
   The ancient towers of Trim ;
And County Meath and Dangan Hall
   They did rewisit him.

I phansy of him so
   His good old thoughts employin' ;
Fourscore years and one ago
   Beside the flowin' Boyne.

His father praps he sees,
   Most musicle of Lords,

A playing maddrigles and glees
  Upon the Arpsicords.

Jest phansy this old Ero
  Upon his mother's knee !
Did ever lady in this land
  Ave greater sons than she !

And I shouldn be surprize
  While this was in his mind,
If a drop there twinkled in his eyes
  Of unfamiliar brind.

    *   *   *   *   *

To Hapsly Ouse next day
  Drives up a Broosh and for,
A gracious prince sits in that Shay
  (I mention him with Hor !)

They ring upon the bell,
  The Porter shows his Ed,
(He fought at Vaterloo as vell,
  And vears a Veskit red).

To see that carriage come,
  The people round it press :
" And is the galliant Duke at ome ?"
  " Your Royal Ighness, yes."

He stepps from out the Broosh
  And in the gate is gone ;
And X, although the people push,
  Says wery kind, " Move hon."

The Royal Prince unto
  The galliant Duke did say,
" Dear Duke, my little son and you
  Was born the self-same day.

" The Lady of the land,
    My wife and Sovring dear,
It is by her horgust command
    I wait upon you here.

" That lady is as well
    As can expected be ;
And to your Grace she bid me tel
    This gracious message free.

" That offspring of our race,
    Whom yesterday you see,
To show our honor for your Grace,
    Prince Arthur he shall be.

" That name it rhymes to fame ;
    All Europe knows the sound :
And I couldn't find a better name
    If you'd give me twenty pound.

" King Arthur had his knights
    That girt his table round,
But you have won a hundred fights,
    Will match 'em, I'll be bound.

" You fought with Bonypart,
    And likewise Tippoo Saib ;
I name you then with all my heart
    The Godsire of this babe."

That Prince his leave was took,
    His hinterview was done.
So let us give the good old Duke
    Good luck of his god-son,

And wish him years of joy
    In this our time of Schism,

And hope he'll hear the royal boy
  His little catechism.

And my pooty little Prince
  That's come our arts to cheer,
Let me my loyal powers ewince
  A welcomin of you ere.

And the Poit-Laureat's crownd,
  I think, in some respex,
Egstremely shootable might be found
  For honest Pleaseman X.

———

THE BALLAD OF ELIZA DAVIS.

GALLIANT gents and lovely ladies,
  List a tail vich late befel,
Vich I heard it, bein on duty,
  At the Pleace Hoffice, Clerkenwell.

Praps you know the Fondling Chapel,
  Vere the little children sings :
(Lor ! I likes to hear on Sundies
  Them there pooty little things !)

In this street there lived a housemaid,
  If you particklarly ask me where—
Vy, it vas at four-and-tventy
  Guilford Street, by Brunsvick Square.

Vich her name was Eliza Davis,
  And she went to fetch the beer :
In the street she met a party
  As was quite surprized to see her.

Vich he vas a British Sailor,
   For to judge him by his look :
Tarry jacket, canvas trowsies,
   Ha-la Mr. T. P. Cooke.

Presently this Mann accostes
   Of this hinnocent young gal—
" Pray," saysee, " excuse my freedom,
   You're so like my Sister Sal !

" You're so like my Sister Sally,
   Both in valk and face and size,
Miss, that—dang my old lee scuppers,
   It brings tears into my heyes !

" I'm a mate on board a wessel,
   I'm a sailor bold and true ;
Shiver up my poor old timbers,
   Let me be a mate for you !

" What's your name, my beauty, tell me ;"
   And she faintly hansers, " Lore,
Sir, my name's Eliza Davis,
   And I live at tventy-four."

Hofttimes came this British seaman,
   This deluded gal to meet ;
And at tventy-four was welcome,
   Tventy-four in Guilford Street.

And Eliza told her Master
   (Kinder they than Misuses are),
How in marridge he had ast her,
   Like a galliant British Tar.

And he brought his landlady vith him,
   (Vich was all his hartful plan),

And she told how Charley Thompson
　Reely vas a good young man :

And how she herself had lived in
　Many years of union sweet
Vith a gent she met promiskous,
　Valkin in the public street.

And Eliza listened to them,
　And she thought that soon their bands
Vould be published at the Fondlin,
　Hand the clergyman jine their ands.

And he ast about the lodgers,
　(Vich her master let some rooms),
Likevise vere they kep their things, and
　Vere her master kep his spoons.

Hand this vicked Charley Thompson
　Came on Sundy veek to see her ;
And he sent Eliza Davis
　Hout to fetch a pint of beer.

Hand while pore Eliza vent to
　Fetch the beer, dewoid of sin,
This etrocious Charley Thompson
　Let his vile accomplish hin.

To the lodgers, their apartments,
　This abandingd female goes,
Prigs their shirts and umberellas ;
　Prigs their boots, and hats, and clothes.

Vile the scoundrle Charley Thompson,
　Lest his wictim should escape,
Hocust her vith rum and vater,
　Like a fiend in huming shape.

But a hi was fixed upon 'em
   Vich these raskles little sore ;
Namely, Mr. Hide, the landlord
   Of the house at tventy-four.

He was valkin in his garden,
   Just afore he vent to sup ;
And on looking up he sor the
   Lodgers' vinders lighted up.

Hup the stairs the landlord tumbled ;
   Something's going wrong, he said ;
And he caught the vicked voman
   Underneath the lodger's bed.

And he called a brother Pleaseman,
   Vich was passing on his beat,
Like a true and galliant feller,
   Hup and down in Guilford Street.

And that Pleaseman able-bodied
   Took this voman to the cell ;
To the cell vere she was quodded,
   In the Close of Clerkenwell.

And though vicked Charley Thompson
   Boulted like a miscrant base,
Presently another Pleaseman
   Took him to the self-same place.

And this precious pair of raskles
   Tuesday last came up for doom ;
By the beak they was committed,
   Vich his name was Mr. Combe.

Has for poor Eliza Davis,
   Simple gurl of tventy-four,

She, I ope, vill never listen
   In the streets to sailors moar.

But if she must ave a sweet-art,
   (Vich most every gurl expex,)
Let her take a jolly pleaseman ;
   Vich his name peraps is—X.

DAMAGES, TWO HUNDRED POUNDS.

SPECIAL Jurymen of England ! who admire your
   country's laws,
And proclaim a British Jury worthy of the realm's
   applause ;
Gayly compliment each other at the issue of a
   cause
Which was tried at Guildford 'sizes this day week
   as ever was.

Unto that august tribunal comes a gentleman in
   grief,
(Special was the British Jury, and the Judge, the
   Baron Chief,)
Comes a British man and husband—asking of the
   law relief,
For his wife was stolen from him—he'd have ven-
   geance on the thief.

Yes, his wife, the blessed treasure with the which
   his life was crowned,
Wickedly was ravished from him by a hypocrite
   profound.
And he comes before twelve Britons, men for
   sense and truth renowned,

To award him for his damage twenty hundred
    sterling pound.

He by counsel and attorney there at Guildford does
    appear,
Asking damage of the villian who seduced his lady
    dear :
But I can't help asking, though the lady's guilt
    was all too clear,
And though guilty the defendant, wasn't the
    plaintiff rather queer ?

First the lady's mother spoke, and said she'd seen
    her daughter cry
But a fortnight after marriage : early times for
    piping eye.
Six months after, things were worse, and the
    piping eye was black,
And this gallant British husband caned his wife
    upon the back.

Three months after they were married, husband
    pushed her to the door,
Told her to be off and leave him, for he wanted
    her no more,
As she would not go, why *he* went : thrice he left
    his lady dear ;
Left her too without a penny, for more than a
    quarter of a year.

Mrs. Frances Duncan knew the parties very well
    indeed,
She had seen him pull his lady's nose and make
    her lip to bleed ;
If he chanced to sit at home not a single word he
    said :
Once she saw him throw the cover of a dish at his
    lady's head.

Sarah Green, another witness, clear did to the
  jury note
How she saw this honest fellow seize his lady by
  the throat,
How he cursed her and abused her, beating her
  into a fit,
Till the pitying next-door neighbors crossed the
  wall and witnessed it.

Next door to this injured Briton Mr. Owers a
  butcher dwelt ;
Mrs. Ower's foolish heart toward this erring
  dame did melt ;
(Not that she had erred as yet, crime was not de-
  veloped in her),
But being left without a penny, Mrs. Owers sup-
  plied her dinner—
God be merciful to Mrs. Owers, who was merciful
  to this sinner !

Caroline Naylor was their servant, said they led a
  wretched life,
Saw this most distinguished Briton fling a teacup
  at his wife ;
He went out to balls and pleasures, and never
  once, in ten months' space,
Sat with his wife or spoke her kindly.   This was
  the defendant's case.

Pollock, C. B., charged the Jury ; said the woman's guilt was clear ;
That was not the point, however, which the Jury
  came to hear ;
But the damage to determine which, as it should
  true appear,
This most tender-hearted husband, who so used
  his lady dear—

Beat her, kicked her, caned her, cursed her, left
    her starving, year by year,
Flung her from him, parted from her, wrung her
    neck, and boxed her ear—
What the reasonable damage this afflicted man
    could claim
By the loss of the affections of this guilty grace-
    less dame ?

Then the honest British Twelve, to each other
    turning round,
Laid their clever heads together with a wisdom
    most profound :
And toward his Lordship looking, spoke the fore-
    man wise and sound ;—
" My Lord, we find for this here plaintiff,
    damages two hundred pound."

So, God bless the Special Jury ! pride and joy of
    English ground,
And the happy land of England, where true jus-
    tice does abound !
British jurymen and husbands, let us hail this
    verdict proper :
If a British wife offends you, Britons, you've a
    right to whop her.

Though you promised to protect her, though you
    promised to defend her,
You are welcome to neglect her : to the devil you
    may send her :
You may strike her, curse, abuse her ; so declares
    our law renowned ;
And if after this you lose her,—why, you're paid
    two hundred pound.

THE KNIGHT AND THE LADY.

There's in the Vest a city pleasant
  To vich King Bladud gev his name,
And in that city there's a Crescent
  Vere dwelt a noble knight of fame.

Although that gallant knight is oldish,
  Although Sir John as grey, grey air,
Hage has not made his busum coldish,
  His Art still beats tewodds the Fair !

'Twas two years sins, this knight so splendid,
  Peraps fateagued with Bath's routines,
To Paris towne his phootsteps bended
  In sutch of gayer folks and scans.

His and was free, his means was easy,
  A nobler, finer gent than he
Ne'er drove about the Shons-Eleesy,
  Or paced the Roo de Rivolee.

A brougham and pair Sir John prowided,
  In which abroad he loved to ride ;
But ar ! he most of all enjyed it,
  When some one helse was sittin' inside !

That " some one helse" a lovely dame was,
  Dear ladies, you will heasy tell—
Countess Grabrowski her sweet name was,
  A noble title, ard to spell.

This faymus Countess ad a daughter
  Of lovely form and tender art ;
A nobleman in marridge sought her,
  By name the Baron of Saint Bart.

Their pashn touched the noble Sir John,
   It was so pewer and profound ;
Lady Grabrowski he did urge on
   With Hyming's wreeth their loves to crownd.

" O, come to Bath, to Lansdowne Crescent,"
   Says kind Sir John, " and live with me ;
The living there's uncommon pleasant—
   I'm sure you'll find the hair agree.

" O, come to Bath, my fair Grabrowski,
   And bring your charming girl," sezee ;
" The Barring here shall have the ouse-key,
   Vith breakfast, dinner, lunch, and tea.

" And when they've passed an appy winter,
   Their opes and loves no more we'll bar ;
The marridge-vow they'll enter inter,
   And I at church will be their Par."

To Bath they went to Lansdowne Crescent,
   Where good Sir John he did provide
No end of teas and balls incessant,
   And hosses both to drive and ride.

He was so Ospitably busy,
   When Miss was late, he'd make so bold
Upstairs to call out, " Missy, Missy,
   Come down, the coffy's getting cold !"

But O ! 'tis sadd to think such bounties
   Should meet with such return as this ;
O Barring of Saint Bart, O Countess
   Grabrowski, and O cruel Miss !

He married you at Bath's fair Habby,
   Saint Bart he treated like a son—
And wasn't it uncommon shabby
   To do what you have went and done

My trembling And amost refewses
　To write the charge which Sir John swore,
Of which the Countess he ecuses,
　Her daughter and her son-in-lore.

My Mews quite blushes as she sings of
　The fatle charge which now I quote :
He says Miss took his two best rings off,
　And pawned 'em for a tenpun note.

" Is this the child of honest parince,
　To make away with folks' best things ?
Is this, pray. like the wives of Barrins,
　To go and prig a gentleman's rings ? "

Thus thought Sir John, by anger wrought on,
　And to rewenge his injured cause,
He brought them hup to Mr. Broughton,
　Last Vensday veek as ever waws.

If guiltless, how she have been slandered !
　If guilty, wengeance will not fail :
Meanwhile the lady is remanded
　And gev three hundred pouns in bail.

JACOB HOMNIUM'S HOSS.

A NEW PALLICE COURT CHAUNT.

One sees in Viteall Yard,
　Vere pleacemen do resort,
A wenerable hinstitute,
　'Tis called the Pallis Court.
A gent as got his i on it,
　I think 'twill make some sport.

The natur of this Court
  My hindignation riles :
A few fat legal spiders
  Here set & spin their viles ;
To rob the town theyr privlege is,
  In a hayrea of twelve miles.

The Judge of this year Court
  Is a mellitary beak,
He knows no more of Lor
  Than praps he does of Greek,
And prowides hisself a deputy
  Because he cannot speak.

Four counsel in this Court—
  Misnamed of Justice—sits ;
These lawyers owes their places to
  There money, not their wits ;
And there's six attornies under them,
  As here their living gits.

These lawyers, six and four,
  Was a living at their ease,
A sendin of their writs abowt,
  And droring in the fees,
When their erose a cirkimstance
  As is like to make a breeze.

It now is some monce since
  A gent both good and trew
Possest an ansum oss vith vich
  He didn know what to do ;
Peraps he did not like the oss,
  Peraps he was a scru.

This gentleman his oss
  At Tattersall's did lodge ;

There came a wulgar oss-dealer.
　This gentleman's name did fodge,
And took the oss from Tattersall's :
　Wasn that a artful dodge ?

One day this gentleman's groom
　This willain did spy out,
A mounted on this oss
　A ridin him about ;
" Get out of that there oss, you rogue,"
Speaks up the groom so stout.

The thief was cruel wex'd
　To find himself so pinn'd ;
The oss began to whinny,
　The honest groom he grinn'd ;
And the raskle thief got off the oss
　And cut avay like vind.

And phansy with what joy
　The master did regard
His dearly bluvd lost oss again
　Trot in the stable yard !

Who was this master good
　Of whomb I makes these rhymes ?
His name is Jacob Homnium, Exquire ;
　And if *I'*d committed crimes,
Good Lord ! I wouldn't ave that mann
　Attack me in the *Times !*

Now shortly after the groomb
　His master's oss did take up,
There came a livery-man
　This gentleman to wake up ;
And he handed in a little bill,
　Which hangered Mr. Jacob.

For two pound seventeen
  This livery-man eplied,
For the keep of Mr. Jacob's oss,
  Which the thief had took to ride.
" Do you see anythink green in me ?"
  Mr. Jacob Homnium cried.

" Because a raskle chews
  My oss away to robb,
And goes tick at your Mews
  For seven-and-fifty bobb,
Shall *I* be call'd to pay ?—It is
  A iniquitious Jobb."

Thus Mr. Jacob cut
  The conwasation short :
The livery-man went ome,
  Detummingd to ave sport,
And summingsd Jacob Homnium, Exquire,
  Into the Pallis Court.

Pore Jacob went to Court,
  A Counsel for to fix,
And choose a barrister out of the four,
  An attorney of the six :
And there he sor these men of Lor,
  And watch'd 'em at their tricks.

The dreadful day of trile
  In the pallis Court did come ;
The lawyers said their say,
  The judge look'd wery glum,
And then the British Jury cast
  Pore Jacob Hom-ni-um.

O a weary day was that
  For Jacob to go through ;

The debt was two seventeen
(Which he no mor owed than you),
And then there was the plaintives costs,
Eleven pound six and two.

And then there was his own,
Which the lawyers they did fix
At a wery moderit figgar
Of ten pound one and six.
Now Evins bless the Pallis Court,
And all its bold ver-dicks !

I cannot settingly tell
If Jacob swaw and cust,
At aving for to pay this sumb ;
But I should think he must,
And av drawn a cheque for £24 4s. 8d.
With most igstreme disgust.

O Pallis Court, you move
My pitty most profound.
A most emusing sport
You thought it I'll be bound,
To saddle hup a three-pound debt
With two and-twenty pound.

Good sport it is to you
To grind the honest pore,
To pay their just or unjust debts
With eight hundred per cent for Lor ;
Make haste and get your costes in,
They will not last much mor !

Come down from that tribewn,
Thou shameless and Unjust ;
Thou Swindle, picking pockets in
The name of Truth august :

Come down, thou hoary Blasphemy,
　For die thou shalt and must.

And go it, Jacob Homnium,
　And ply your iron pen,
And rise up, Sir John Jervis,
　And shut me up that den ;
That sty for fattening lawyers in
　On the bones of honest men.

PLEACEMAN X.

———

THE SPECULATORS.

THE night was stormy and dark, 　The town was shut up in sleep : Only those were abroad who were out on a lark, 　Or those who'd no beds to keep.

I pass'd through the lonely street, 　The wind did sing and blow ; I could hear the policeman's feet 　Clapping to and fro.

There stood a potato-man 　In the midst of all the wet ; He stood with his 'tato-can 　In the lonely Haymarket.

Two gents of dismal mien, 　And dank and greasy rags, 　Came out of a shop for gin, 　Swaggering over the flags :

Swaggering over the stones, 　These shabby bucks did walk ; And I went and followed those seedy ones, 　And listened to their talk.

Was I sober or awake ?   Could I believe my
ears ?   Those dismal beggars spake   Of nothing
but railroad shares.

I wondered more and more :   Says one —
" Good friend of mine,   How many shares have
you wrote for,   In the Diddlesex Junction line ?"

" I wrote for twenty," says Jim,   " But they
wouldn't give me one ;"   His comrade straight
rebuked him   For the folly he had done :

" O Jim, you are unawares   Of the ways of
this bad town ;   *I* always write for five hundred
shares,   And *then* they put me down."

" And yet you got no shares,"   Says Jim, " for
all your boast ;"   " I *would* have wrote," says
Jack, " but where   Was the penny to pay the
post ?"

" I lost, for I couldn't pay   That first instal-
ment up ;   But here's 'taters smoking hot—I say,
Let's stop, my boy, and sup."

And at this simple feast   The while they did
regale,   I drew each ragged capitalist   Down on
my left thumb-nail.

Their talk did me perplex,   All night I tumbled
and tost,   And thought of railroad specs,   And
how money was won and lost.

" Bless railroads everywhere," I said, " and
the world's advance ;   Bless every railroad share
In Italy, Ireland, France ;   For never a beggar
need now despair,   And every rogue has a
chance."

A WOEFUL NEW BALLAD

OF THE

PROTESTANT CONSPIRACY TO TAKE THE POPE'S LIFE.

(BY A GENTLEMAN WHO HAS BEEN ON THE SPOT.)

COME all ye Christian people, unto my tale give
ear,
'Tis about a base consperracy, as quickly shall
appear;
'Twill make your hair to bristle up, and your eyes
to start and glow,
When of this dread consperracy you honest folks
shall know.

The news of this consperracy and villianous
attempt,
I read it in a newspaper, from Italy it was sent:
It was sent from lovely Italy, where the olives
they do grow,
And our Holy Father lives, yes, yes, while his
name it is No NO.

And 'tis there our English noblemen goes that is
Puseyites no longer,
Because they finds the ancient faith both better
is and stronger.
And 'tis there I knelt beside my lord when he
kiss'd the POPE his toe,
And hung his neck with chains at Saint Peter's
Vinculo.

And 'tis there the splendid churches is, and the
fountains playing grand,
And the palace of PRINCE TORLONIA, likewise
the Vatican:

And there's the stairs where the bagpipe-men and
the piffararys blow.
And it's there I drove my lady and lord in the
Park of Pincio.

And 'tis there our splendid churches is in all their
pride and glory,
Saint Peter's famous Basilisk and Saint Mary's
Maggiory ;
And them benighted Prodestants, on Sunday they
must go
Outside the town to the preaching-shop by the
gate of Popolo.

Now in this town of famous Room, as I dessay
you have heard,
There is scarcely any gentleman as hasn't got a
· beard.
And ever since the world began it was ordained so,
That there should always barbers be wheresumever
beards do grow.

And as it always has been so since the world it
did begin,
The POPE, our Holy Potentate, has a beard upon
his chin ;   ·
And every morning regular when cocks begin to
crow,
There comes a certing party to wait on POPE PIO.

There comes a certing gintleman with razier, soap,
and lather,
A shaving most respectfully the POPE, our Holy
Father.
And now the dread consperracy I'll quickly to you
show,
Which them sanguinary Prodestants did form
against NONO.

Them sanguinary Prodestants, which I abore and
 hate,
Assembled in the preaching-shop by the Flaminian
 gate ;
And they took counsel with their selves to deal a
 deadly blow
Against our gentle Father, the Holy Pope Pio.

Exhibiting a wickedness which I never heerd or
 read of ;
What do you think them Prodestants wished ? to
 cut the good Pope's head off !
And to the kind Pope's Air-dresser the Prodestant
 Clark did go,
And proposed him to decapitate the innocent
 Pio.

" What hever can be easier," said this Clerk—this
 Man of Sin,
" When you are called to hoperate on His Holi-
 ness's chin,
Than just to give the razier a little slip—just so ?—
And there's an end, dear barber, of innocent Pio !"

This wicked conversation it chanced was overerd
By an Italian lady ; she heard it every word :
Which by birth she was a Marchioness, in service
 forced to go
With the parson of the preaching-shop at the gate
 of Popolo.

When the lady heard the news, as duty did obleege,
As fast as her legs could carry her she ran to the
 Poleege.
" O Polegia," says she (for they pronounts it so),
" They're going for to massyker our Holy Pope
 Pio.

" The ebomminable Englishmen, the Parsing and
  his Clark,
His Holiness's Air-dresser devised it in the dark !
And I would recommend you in prison for to
  throw
These villians would esassinate the Holy Pope
  Pio !

" And for saving of His Holiness and his trebble
  crownd
I humbly hope your Worships will give me a
  few pound ;
Because I was a Marchioness many years ago,
Before I came to service at the gate of Popolo."

That sackreligious Air-dresser, the Parson and
  his man,
Wouldn't though ask'd continyally, own their
  wicked plan—
And so the kind Authoraties let those villians go
That was plotting of the murder of the good Pio
  Nono.

Now isn't this safishnt proof, ye gentlemen at
  home,
How wicked is them Prodestants, and how good
  our Pope at Rome ;
So let us drink confusion to LORD JOHN and
  LORD MINTO,
And a health unto His Eminence, and good Poi
  Nono.

THE LAMENTABLE BALLAD OF THE FOUNDLING OF SHOREDITCH.

COME all ye Christian people, and listen to my
  tail,
It is all about a doctor was travelling by the rail,
By the Heastern Counties' Railway (vich the
  shares I don't desire),
From Ixworth town in Suffolk, vich his name did
  not transpire.

A travelling from Bury this Doctor was employed
With a gentleman, a friend of his, vich his name
  was Captain Loyd,
And on reaching Marks Tey Station, that is next
  beyond Colchest-
er, a lady entered in to them most elegantly
  dressed.

She entered into the Carriage all with a tottering
  step,
And a pooty little Bayby upon her bussum slep ;
The gentlemen received her with kindness and
  siwillaty,
Pitying this lady for her illness and debillaty.

She had a fust-class ticket, this lovely lady said ;
Because it was so lonesome she took a secknd
  instead.
Better to travel by secknd class, than sit alone in
  the fust,
And the pooty little Baby upon her breast she
  nust.

A scein of her cryin, and shiverin and pail,
To her spoke this surging, the Ero of my tail ;

Saysee you look unwell, Ma'am, I'll elp you if I
   can,
And you may tell your case to me, for I'm a
   meddicle man.

" Thank you, Sir," the lady said, " I only look so
   pale,
Because I ain't accustom'd to travelling on the
   Kale ;
I shall be better presnly, when I've ad some
   rest :"
And that pooty little Baby she squeeged it to her
   breast.

So in conwersation the journey they beguiled,
Capting Loyd and the meddicle man, and the lady
   and the child,
Till the warious stations along the line was passed,
For even the Heastern Counties' trains must come
   in at last.

When at Shoreditch tumminus at lenth stopped
   the train,
This kind meddicle gentleman proposed his aid
   again.
" Thank you, Sir," the lady said, " for your kyind-
   ness dear ;
My carridge and my osses is probibbly come here.

" Will you old this baby, please, vilst I step and
   see ?"
The Doctor was a famly man : " That I will,"
   says he.
Then the little child she kist, kist it very gently,
Vich was sucking his little fist, sleeping inno-
   cently.

With a sigh from her art, as though she would
    have bust it,
Then she gave the Doctor the child—wery kind
    he nust it :
Hup then the lady jumped hoff the bench she sat
    from,
Tumbled down the carridge steps and ran along
    the platform.

Vile hall the other passengers vent upon their
    vays,
The Capting and the Doctor sat there in a maze ;
Some vent in a Homminibus, some vent in a
    Cabby,
The Capting and the Doctor vaited vith the babby.

There they sat looking queer, for an hour or
    more,
But their feller passinger neather on 'em sore :
Never, never back again did that lady come
To that pooty sleeping Hinfnt a suckin of his
    Thum !

What could this pore Doctor do, bein treated thus,
When the darling Baby woke, cryin for its nuss ?
Off he drove to a female friend, vich she was
    both kind and mild,
And igsplained to her the circumstance of this
    year little child.

That kind lady took the child instantly in her lap,
And made it very comfortable by giving it some
    pap ;
And when she took its close off, what d'you think
    she found ?
A couple of ten pun notes sewn up, in its little
    gownd !

Also in its little close was a note which did conwey,
That this little baby's parents lived in a hand-
    some way
And for its Headucation they reglarly would pay,
And sirtingly like gentlefolks would claim the
    child one day,
If the Christian people who'd charge of it would
    say,
Per adwertisement in *The Times*, where the baby
    lay.

Pity of this bayby many people took,
It had such pooty ways and such a pooty look ;
And there came a lady forrard (I wish that I
    could see
Any kind lady as would do as much for me ;

And I wish with all my art, some night in *my*
    night gownd,
I could find a note stitched for ten or twenty
    pound)—
There came a lady forrard, that most honorable
    did say,
She'd adopt this little baby, which her parents
    cast away.

While the Doctor pondered on this hoffer fair,
Comes a letter from Devonshire, from a party
    there,
Hordering the Doctor, at its Mar's desire,
To send the little Infant back to Devonshire.

Lost in apoplexity, this pore meddicle man,
Like a sensable gentleman, to the Justice ran ;
Which his name was Mr. Hammill, a honorable
    beak,
That takes his seat in Worship Street four times
    a week.

"O Justice !" says the Doctor, "instrugt me
  what to do.
I've come up from the country, to throw myself
  on you ;
My patients have no doctor to tend them in their
  ills,
(There they are in Suffolk without their draffts
  and pills !)

" I've come up from the country, to know how
  I'll dispose
Of this pore little baby, and the twenty pun note,
  and the close,
And I want to go back to Suffolk, dear Justice, if
  you please,
And my patients wants their Doctor, and their
  Doctor wants his feez."

Up spoke Mr. Hammill, sittin at his desk,
" This year application does me much perplesk ;
What I do adwise you, is to leave this babby
In the Parish where it was left by its mother
  shabby."

The Doctor from his Worship sadly did depart—
He might have left the baby, but he hadn't got
  the heart
To go for to leave that Hinnocent, has the laws
  allows,
To the tender mussies of the Union House.

Mother, who left this little one on a stranger's
  knee,
Think how cruel you have been, and how good
  was he !
Think, if you've been guilty, innocent was she ;
And do not take unkindly this little word of me :
Heaven be merciful to us all, sinners as we be !

THE ORGAN-BOY'S APPEAL.

"Westminster Police Court.—Policeman X brought
a paper of doggerel verses to the Magistrate, which had
been thrust into his hands, X said, by an Italian boy, who
ran away immediately afterward.

"The Magistrate, after perusing the lines, looked
hard at X, and said he did not think they were written by
an Italian.

"X, blushing, said he thought the paper read in
Court last week, and which frightened so the old gentleman to whom it was addressed, was also not of Italian
origin."

O Signor Broderip, you are a wickid ole man,
You wexis us little horgin-boys whenever you
    can :
How dare you talk of Justice, and go for to seek
To pussicute us horgin-boys, you senguinary
    Beek?

Though you set in Vestminster surrounded by
    your crushers,
Harrogint and habsolute like the Hortacrat of
    hall the Rushers,
Yet there is a better vurld I'd have you for to
    know,
Likewise a place vere the henimies of horgin-boys
    will go.

O you vickid Herod without any pity !
London vithout horgin-boys vood be a dismal city.
Sweet Saint Cicily who first taught horgin-
    pipes to blow
Soften the heart of this Magistrit that haggery-
    wates us so !

Good Italian gentlemen, fatherly and kind,
Brings us over to London here our horgins for to
    grind ;

Sends us out vith little vite mice and guinea-pigs
    also
A popping of the Veasel and a Jumpin of JIM
    CROW.

And as us young horgin-boys is grateful in our
    turn
We gives to these kind gentlemen hall the money
    we earn,
Because that they vood vop us as wery wel we
    know
Unless we brought our hurnings back to them as
    loves us so.

O MR. BRODERIP! wery much I'm surprise,
Ven you take your valks abroad where can be
    your eyes?
If a Beak had a heart then you'd compryend
Us pore little horgin-boys was the poor man's
    friend.

Don't you see the shildren in the droring-rooms
Clapping of their little ands when they year our
    toons?
On their mothers' bussums don't you see the
    babbies crow
And down to us dear horgin-boys lots of apence
    throw?

Don't you see the ousemaids (pooty POLLIES and
    MARIES),
Ven ve bring our urdigurdis, smiling from the
    hairies?
Then they come out vith a slice o' cole puddn or
    a bit o' bacon or so
And give it us young horgin-boys for lunch afore
    we go.

Have you ever seen the Hirish children sport
When our velcome music-box brings sunshine in
  the Court?
To these little paupers who can never pay
Surely all good horgin-boys, for GOD's love, will
  play.

Has for those proud gentlemen, like a serting
  B—k
(Vich I von't be pussonal and therefore vil not
  speak),
That flings their parler-vinders hup ven ve begin
  to play
And cusses us and swears at us in such a wiolent
  way,

Instedd of their abewsing and calling hout Poleece
Let em send out JOHN to us vith sixpence or a
  shillin apiece.
Then like good young horgin-boys avay from
  there we'll go,
Blessing sweet SAINT CICILY that taught our
  pipes to blow.

FINIS.